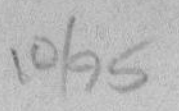

Danger at the Annual Anticrime & Detection Equipment Trade Show

"Permit me, don't y'know, to introduce myself," said the mechanical man in his lazy, cultured voice. "Inspector Volto here, the latest criminological breakthrough of the respected Forentech Corporation of Murdstone."

Molly took Volto's sales booklet, but didn't open it. She stood studying the seated android, tapping the booklet on her chin. "What are your weapons?"

Inspector Volto smiled and stood. "I'm most pleased you asked that question," he said, turning toward Jolson. "By the bye, old man, you are Ben Jolson of the Briggs Interplanetary Detective Service, are you not?"

"Part time, sure," answered Jolson. "But how come you—"

"Allow me to bid you a fond farewell." There was a kilgun in the android's hand and it was swinging toward Jolson. "You'll never take this new case, old boy."

The Exchameleon Series
by Ron Goulart
Published in paperback by St. Martin's Press

DAREDEVILS, LTD.

The Exchameleon Book 2

Starpirate's Brain

RON GOULART

ST. MARTIN'S PRESS/NEW YORK

STARPIRATE'S BRAIN

Library of Congress Catalog Card Number: 87-60650

ISBN: 0-312-90053-8 Can. ISBN: 0-312-90764-8

Printed in the United States of America

First edition/October 1987

10 9 8 7 6 5 4 3 2 1

CHAPTER 1

Things hadn't been going all that well even before the android tried to kill him.

For instance, Ben Jolson didn't particularly want to be attending this Annual Anticrime and Detection Equipment Trade Show in the first place. And the tall, lanky Jolson hadn't been in the Grand Pinnacle Ballroom of the Ritz-Plaza more than two minutes when a gorillaman stepped on his foot.

"You ought to watch where you plant them gunboats of yours, sport," the tuxsuited gorilla said in his gruff, whispery voice. "I didn't come all the way here to Barnum to get my dogs tromped on."

"Excuse it, I mistook you for a part of the decor."

"Say, is that a veiled wisecrack or—"

"Honestly, Ben," said pretty red-haired Molly Briggs, tugging at his arm. "You'll have to excuse my associate, sir. He's a grouch."

"We'll let it pass this time, lady," whispered the gorilla. Tipping his homburg, he moved away into the milling crowd.

"We're here," reminded Molly, "to take in all these

terrific displays of the very latest in crimebusting gadgetry. Not to trade punches with innocent bystand—"

"The guy tromped on my foot," said Jolson as the young woman hustled him toward a booth. "I was a model of cordial, self-effacing behavior."

"The trouble with you," she told him, "is that you're not enthusiastic enough about your chosen profession."

"My chosen profession is the ceramics business. In a moment of weakness I signed up to work for your detective agency on a limited part-time basis, but—"

"Dad had one of his new lawbots scan your contract again only the other day, Ben, and we think—if you interpret certain clauses in certain ways—that maybe what you really signed up for was a modified full-time situation with—"

"Nope, no." He halted in front of a booth presided over by two portly catman representatives of Dorammer, Inc. "The Briggs Interplanetary Detective Service only gets me now and again. I shouldn't even have allowed you to cajole me into attending this nitwit trade show."

"Give it a try, sir." Smiling, one of the catmen dropped a fat orange pistol into his hand.

"What is it?"

"See, Leonard," said the other catman, shaking his furry head. "I told you we don't have sufficient product identification."

His partner pointed a fuzzy finger at the glosign floating above their small plaz-walled booth. "Note our sign, sir. Note the object you are now about to sample," he said. "I assume you're in some branch of the detectival trade and therefore are capable of deducing what—"

"It's a portable door rammer," explained the other catman.

"He was on the verge of guessing that for himself, Merle." The first catman glowered. "Now shake a leg and set up another door."

"Do you know what these darn doors cost? And, you'll excuse my saying, this gink doesn't look like he's got the wherewithal to buy an expensive—"

"You're not utilizing your own deductive abilities, Merle. Gander his titian-haired companion, if you will."

"Ah, she's obviously moneyed."

Molly lifted the pistol off Jolson's palm. "What's this thing supposed to do?"

"The Dorammer is perfect for raids on thieves' dens, intrusions on errant spouses in seedy skytels," said Leonard. "As well as sundry and other everyday crimestopping occasions. You simply aim it at yonder door, squeeze the easy-to-squeeze trigger and—"

"What door?" Molly hefted the gun, sighted along the barrel.

"Merle, didn't I tell you to set one up?"

The other catman scooted around to the rear of their booth, made grunting noises and then appeared inside the booth worrying a three-panel neowood door into place. "I'll lean it against the wall here, miss," he said, puffing. "You must imagine that it's actually an impregnable portal of—"

"She can do that, Merle. Clear out."

Molly waited until the catman left the booth, then aimed the orange gun. "We might want to equip all our operatives with these, Ben. They're sort of cute, don't you think?"

"Fetching," he said.

"Okay, here goes." She pulled the trigger.

The demonstration-model gun produced a jittery fizzling sound.

"Excuse me a moment, miss." Leonard retrieved his gun, whapped it on the side several times with the heel of his paw.

Zzzzzmmmmmmooooookkkkkkk!

A skinny beam of sizzling green light erupted out of the barrel, shot up and ate most of the Dorammer sign.

"That costs three times as much as a door," lamented Merle, sawdust drifting down on his furry head.

Sighing, Molly urged Jolson onward. "There's something else I want to talk to you about."

"Besides my servitude to BIDS?"

"This has to do with our recent case out in the Hellquad planets." She dodged a servobot who was going by with a tray of tiny kelp sandwiches. "We worked together very well, no denying that. In a business sort of way is what I mean."

"Teamwork," said Jolson, "is what we evidenced, yes."

"The point is, well, I maybe became a bit, you know, emotional."

"I didn't notice."

"Sure you did. I mean, I was kissing you and acting like a darn kid instead of a mature woman of twenty-six who—"

"Twenty-eight."

"I really wish, once in a while, you'd let me fudge." She sighed again. "Anyway, Ben, I think I probably behaved in a sort of dippy fashion. What with all those murders going on and crazed androids chasing us and . . . well, I feel we ought to be just friends from now on."

He nodded. "A judicious decision."

Molly scowled. "You know, sometimes you really make me exceptionally angry with that aloof act. What I mean is, here I'm telling you that what might've been a great romance must, for practical business reasons, be curtailed until—"

"Gruel."

A plump, motherly robot had rolled into their path. She had the words *Mrs. Mush* emblazoned on both her round forehead and her ample metallic bosom. A kettle of steaming gruel was built into her stomach.

The robot was in the act of spooning out a free sample bowl of mush. "No, thanks." said Jolson.

"Let's take a look at that field andy over there," suggested Molly.

"You two tykes ought not to pass up a nutritious heart-warming bowl of Mrs. Mush's gruel," called the motherly robot. "It contains your minimum daily requirements of everything."

"Here, folks, stop here," hailed a grinning frogman in a two-piece yellow glosuit. "Try our new compact MicroStun stunrod out. Yes, and try it on a real living, breathing human. For extra fun, every one of these especially hired raggedy welfs you hit will topple like a plummet from his or her chair and into a tub of chill water. Lots of laughs as well as a surefire demonstration of the capabilities—"

"I wonder about some of our colleagues," said Molly.

"You and me both, sister." A small glittering robot dog

was eying her from around the edge of a Minibug Spy System booth.

"What a cute toy," she said, crouching.

"Knock it off, I'm no toy," said the dog, his plaz eyes flaring red for a few angry seconds. "I happen to be one of the most sophisticated trackers in this corner—or any corner, for that matter—of this benighted universe. Not only that, I'm also a crackerjack investigator, and I contain a built-in forensic lab along with—"

"You don't need a pet," said Jolson.

"Take a hike, beanpole," suggested the dog. "Who is this lunkhead, sister? One of your retainers?"

"Don't be nasty to Ben," she advised the robot animal. "Because if I bought you, you'd have to get along with all of our operatives and—"

"This dimbulb is an op?" The chrome-plated robot dog snickered, rolled his eyes, wagged his springy silver tail in a derisive way. "He couldn't find his own backside in the dark without help."

"What do the basic laws of robotics have to say about booting a wiseass?" asked Jolson.

"Red, why don't you ditch this emaciated goon and trot over to my booth?" suggested the dog, winking up at Molly. "See it over the way there, Sniffer, Inc.? 'Unquestionably the Best Electronic Police Dog in the Universe!' I'm not dead certain our slogan is forceful enough for the kind of yokels we have to deal with at this—"

"I'll drop in on you before we leave," she promised, patting him on his slick silvery head as he rose.

"One thing, kiddo," cautioned Sniffer. "I allowed you to pat me this once, but if I work for you there's to be no more patronizing gestures. We're equals." Turning his glittering rear to them, he went trotting away through the crowd.

"Sort of sweet, for all his bluster," she said. "I might order one or two. A Sniffer would brighten up the—"

"What say we continue our tour."

Molly took his arm again. "Sometimes I find it hard to believe you were in the Chameleon Corps for ages and ages," she said. "Since it is a branch of Barnum's Political Espionage Office, they should've taught you—"

"Twenty years isn't ages and ages."

"Should've taught you a little diplomacy. What I mean is, getting along with even a lowly robot puppy is the mark of a true diplomat," Molly said. "Also, you needn't be so sensitive about your age. After all, forty-five isn't actually old. Well, it's old, but not ancient—"

"Forty-two."

She shrugged her left shoulder. "Here's the android I'm especially interested in."

An oval pedestal rose three feet above the mosaic plaz floor of the vast ballroom. Atop it a Lucite rocking chair ticked gently back and forth. Seated in the chair was a handsome, aquiline-visaged humanoid mechanical man in a conservative three-piece neotweed bizsuit.

"Permit me, don't y'know, to introduce myself," he said in his lazy, cultured voice. "Inspector Volto here, the latest criminological breakthrough of the respected Foren-Tech Corporation of Murdstone."

"Pleased to meet you." Slowly Molly circled the rocking android.

"Why so bloomin' glum, old boy?" the inspector asked Jolson.

"See if you can deduce the reasons." Jolson thrust his hands into the slashpockets of his trousers.

"All I know, lad, is that I'd be deuced jolly were I escortin' such a perishin' handsome lady as you have in tow." He reached inside his nubby jacket. "You might, fair lady, peruse this enlightenin' little booklet, which outlines the one hundred and one advantages that Inspector Volto has over comparable field investigator androids on the market."

Molly took the booklet but didn't open it. She stood studying the seated android, tapping the booklet on her chin. "What about weapons?"

Inspector Volto smiled and stood. "I'm most pleased you asked that question," he said, turning toward Jolson. "By the by, old man, you are Ben Jolson of the Briggs Interplanetary Detective Service, are you not?"

"Part-time, sure," answered Jolson. "But how come you—"

"Allow me to bid you a fond farewell." There was a kilgun in the android's hand and it was swinging toward Jolson.

CHAPTER 2

Jolson did two things at once. He dived for the floor and he reached under his jacket for his stungun.

"You'll never take this new case, old boy."

Zzzzzitttzzzzz!

The shimmering scarlet beam of Inspector Volto's kilgun hit dead center on the spot where Jolson had been a few seconds earlier.

Acrid blackish smoke came swirling up and a plate-sized chunk of ballroom floor ceased to be.

Jolson rolled against a servobot, tipping him sideways.

A silver platter of groutballs and snerg rinds spun out of the bot's coppery clutches, went pinwheeling into the retreating bystanders.

Zzzzzzummmmmmm!

Getting off a shot, Jolson scurried to a new position behind the side wall of a Truthjuice booth.

The stunbeam slammed into the android inspector's chest. He swayed, eyes commencing to blink rapidly. But he didn't fall. "Feelin' deuced odd," he admitted in a fuzzy mutter, firing again, with his gun hand quivering now.

Zzzzzitttzzzz!

His shot came nowhere near Jolson, but it did slice a dozen sample plazflasks of Truthjuice in half and sent the blue liquid splashing over retreating bystanders and the lean birdman running the booth.

"You really have to quit behaving this way," said Molly, angry. She'd tugged a lazgun free of her thigh holster. "What I mean is, I hate to ruin a costly mechanism, but you can't go killing one of our operatives."

Zzzzzaaaattttttt!

Her first blast snipped the inspector's right arm clean off.

"I say, old girl, this little squabble's betwixt myself and the Jolson bloke. No need for you to—"

Zzzzzzatttttttt!

The second shot from Molly's small ebony gun swiftly sliced off the top of Inspector Volto's head.

"Ah, alas," he murmured. "Afraid it's all up with . . ."

He went falling back into his rocking chair.

The chair rocked to and fro, faster and faster. Then it somersaulted off the pedestal.

Inspector Volto left the chair when it smacked the floor. He flipped over on his side and lay still. His right hand sprung open, the kilgun slid away.

"Let me tell you folks something," said the Truthjuice booth operator. "In fact, I feel compelled to tell one and all that this stuff is vastly overpriced. Heck, we can make gallons of it for a few trucents and yet—"

"Just a mo, meathead," said a dogman, who'd also been splashed with the bluish fluid. "I don't usually voice my honest opinions like this, but this time it's different. We're supposed to be so tolerant of others, but that's all swill. Birdmen are disgusting, feathery dunks who ought . . ."

Jolson made his way to the fallen android. Genuflecting, he probed into the open skull with his forefinger. "Thanks for the assist," he said to Molly.

She crouched beside him, touched his back tentatively. "Their brochure reads great, but I guess there are a few kinks in the Inspector Voltos," she said. "You all right?"

"Splendid." He located what he was searching for inside the metal skull of the defunct inspector. "Here's what made Volto act up," he said, holding out a small green disc.

"A parasite control disc," she said, taking it.

"Looks to be of off-planet manufacture," he said.

"From the planet Esmeralda, you twit." The robot dog shoved his way through the gathering watchers, plaz nose vibrating slightly. "You can tell by the tiny red dot on its underbelly, which is the trademark of—"

"How'd you see that from way over there?" asked Molly.

"Telescopic vision," replied Sniffer. "Only one of my many advanced attachments."

Taking the disc back, Jolson dropped it into a pocket. "Let's depart," he told the redhead. "We have to converse."

Her eyes widened some. "About what?"

"The late inspector mentioned, in the course of his assassination attempt, a new case I am supposed to be at work on," Jolson said. "Since I wasn't aware of any assignment, that's the first topic we'll go into, Molly."

"Well, there does happen to be a new case that my father and I think you're just about perfect for," admitted the young woman. "I was intending to bring it up, but you've been so grumpy thus far that—"

"Listen, sister," said Sniffer, "any case this bonehead can handle, I can tackle. And I won't let any clunky andies shoot me up either. The Sniffer folks are having a special trade show sale and you can pick me up for a song. Plus which, you'll get a rebate of two thousand trubux."

"That's twice as much as I'd pay for you," Jolson said. "Now scoot. Go chase a mechanical cat."

"I'll pixphone *you* later, Miss Briggs." Sniffing, the dog took his leave.

Molly watched Sniffer growl his way back to his booth. "He *is* sort of appealing," she said thoughtfully. "Did you happen to notice his price?"

"Beyond your means," answered Jolson.

Resting his buttocks against the edge of the neowood desk in one of the BIDS offices, Jolson nodded at the computer terminal floating a few feet away. "What else?"

The terminal shrugged. "That's all, Benny."

"Ben," he corrected as he reread the material on the screen. "No prints or aura traces on the parasite used to take over Inspector Volto. Gadget itself purchased anonymously three days ago in the capital city of Jazinto Territory on the planet Esmeralda in our Barnum System. Nothing on who planted it or when."

"We're working on that, Benjamin," said the voxbox of the terminal. "And we'll get a copy of the Municops report on the whole incident. They, let me add, are miffed that you and Molly didn't linger at the scene of the crime until—"

"Lingering places where somebody's trying to do me in makes me—"

"Well, okay," said Molly as she came into the office, "I'm all set to brief you on your next job for the detective agency, Ben."

"He prefers to be called Benjamin," mentioned the floating terminal.

"He doesn't. Go away."

Shrugging again, the terminal drifted out through the still-open doorway. The pale yellow panel whispered shut.

Molly unburdened herself of the armload of faxbooks, infospools, file folders, memos and plyopackets she'd been carrying. The stuff sprawled across the desktop. "What more have you found out about the attempts on our lives?"

"My life."

"Nope, I really think that berserk andy meant to rub me out once he'd—"

"The parasite's instruction code called for him to kill only me." He left the desk and moved to one of the high, wide one-way viewindows. "Somebody on Esmeralda had the idea I was coming out there. They attempted to discourage me."

"But hardly anyone knew you might be scheduled to—"

"Not even I knew. When were you planning to—"

"At lunch. Except what with that mechanical man shooting up the . . . Oh, and that reminds me. Do you want the soy loaf on white or fakeham on sudorye?"

"Neither."

"C'mon, you can't get briefed on an empty stomach." Molly held up the two plyowrapped sandwiches. "Pick."

"What's that oozing out of the ham sandwich?"

"Mayo."

"It's blue."

"The delibot explained that to me. Seems their saucier was stricken suddenly color-blind and they haven't gotten around to—"

"I'll take the soy loaf." Accepting the sandwich, Jolson turned his attention to the view outside. The afternoon was clear and bright, and the multicolored towers and pastel pedramps of the capital city of Barnum's largest territory rose all around.

"We do have other ex-Chameleons on the staff," began Molly, unwrapping her fakeham. "Well, heck, there's my father, for one. But of all our operatives who possess the ability to change shape and assume other identities, you, Ben, are the fellow I think is best suited for this particular detective chore."

"Oh, does it require a gullible half-wit?"

"You aren't a gullible half-wit."

"I'd have to be to take an assignment where I know in advance somebody's out to exterminate me."

Nose wrinkling, Molly poked her forefinger into the heart of her sandwich. "I guess there's nothing basically wrong with mayonnaise the color of the deep blue sea, and yet . . . Ben, now that we know there's extra danger, we can prepare for it."

"And charge a higher fee."

Molly nodded slowly. "Well, yes, that, too."

He left the window, came around to face her. "Who's the client?"

"You're certain to like her, being as you're somewhat artistic yourself."

"She's in ceramics too?"

"No, Maybelle Vexford is an author." Boosting herself up onto the desk and crossing her long handsome legs, Molly rummaged through the scatter of stuff. "Here's one of her books. *The Great History of Space Piracy.* Fourteen weeks on the Esmeralda *News-Times*' Best-Seller List, alternate selection of the—"

"What's she want BIDS to do?"

"Find someone."

"You don't need a former Chameleon Corps agent for a simple missing person—"

"This isn't exactly simple, Ben."

He joined her atop the desk. "Explain."

Molly tapped the cover of the faxbook. "Oops, got mayo on the darn jacket. At any rate, Maybelle Vexford is one of the leading authoresses on the whole planet of Esmeralda—a rather dowdy birdwoman, judging by this picture of her on the back of the book. Her specialty is fact crime, mostly the vicious and rotten doings of space pirates and looters."

"Has Maybelle lost a pirate?"

Molly brushed at her long red hair. "Well, only part of one, actually."

CHAPTER 3

"His *brain?*" asked Jolson, glancing from the wall viewscreen to Molly.

"Well, sort of." Her long red hair brushed her shoulders as she nodded at the nearly life-size image on the wall in front of them. "Let me give you a bit more information about Jackland Boggs."

Boggs was a large green-skinned man. His hair was a dusty bronze color, and his crinkly beard reached to the middle of his broad chest. Hands on hips, he stood snarling at the camera. His drooping gunbelt held a kilgun and a stungun. A wicked-bladed knife was gripped in his jagged teeth.

"This picture obviously isn't from his college yearbook," commented Jolson.

"It's a publicity photo. You see, Boggs has carried on a highly successful career as a space pirate, a looter of spaceliners, a pillager of skymines and star colonies. His various activities in those areas have earned him the nickname of—"

"Starpirate," said Jolson, snapping his fingers in recognition. "Sure, he was active when I was still in the Chameleon Corps."

"Supposedly Starpirate retired a couple of years ago," said the young woman. "Some kind of deal was worked out and he was allowed to retire and reside peacefully on the planet Esmeralda. Except he—"

"Didn't quite retire," said Jolson. "Not more than two months back Boggs raided the spaceyacht of a gent named Miguelito Saticoy. Saticoy was the impressively crooked prime minister of one of the big territories on Esmeralda. When Starpirate waylaid him, he was en route to a comfortable exile on Barafunda. Carrying loot rumored to be worth a little over six billion trudollars, as well as a half-dozen tubby wives and vox and fax records of the various and sundry crooked deals he'd entered into during a fruitful twelve-year reign."

"Darn."

"What's the matter?"

"Well, you've just recited what was going to be the next segment of the briefing." She shifted in her slingchair. "This was supposed to be highly confidential data."

"I still hear things."

"Do you want to see a picture of Prime Minister Saticoy?"

"Not especially."

"Or his wives in their glogowns at an Antifamine Banquet and Dance? There are seven of them, actually."

"Not at all." He dropped from the desk, began pacing the darkened room. "What I still don't know is how Boggs's brain happens to be missing."

Molly brightened. "Oh, good, then there's something I

can still fill you in on." Stretching, she flipped a toggle on the desk and a new picture popped up on the wall. "Gosh, is that upside down?"

"Fellow's standing on his head."

"Well, that makes sense. He's a doctor, and obviously interested in physical fitness."

Jolson cocked his head, squinted at the pudgy headstanding catman. "That's Dr. Albert J. Chowderman," he said. "Well-known electrosurgeon, also a resident of Esmeralda. How's he fit in?"

"The doctor recently perfected a procedure—very costly—whereby the entire contents of a brain can be transferred electronically, and painlessly, to a dinky neosilicon chip," she explained, consulting a faxmemo. "Once the information is switched, though, the original organic brain is left totally empty. What Dr. Chowderman does then is implant the chip back in the patient's skull and all is well. Except you have to wait a few days after the transfer before hooking up the chip."

Jolson paused in front of the image of the furry physician. "Chowderman performed a switch for Starpirate?"

"That's it, yes."

"Why?"

"Turns out Jackland Boggs was suffering from a rare ailment known as Ellison's syndrome," she answered. "Victims find that their brains go completely and permanently blank in a matter of months. His only hope was the Chowderman process. And, what with all his old pirate loot hidden away hither and yon, he could well afford the price tag."

"So Chowderman switched the contents of his brain to a chip?"

"That's right, but then—"

"The chip disappeared."

"A few hours after the transfer, and long before it was time to implant it, persons unknown broke into the doctor's prestigious electroclinic and made off with the darn thing," said Molly. "Leaving poor Boggs with no brain at all."

"All the gent who swiped it has to do is slip it into a brainbox and he can find out everything Starpirate knows." Jolson grinned. "Where all the plunder is hidden, where all the incriminating political material is stashed."

"Yes, and that's why I think you're going to have competition out there on Esmeralda." Molly flicked off the wall image and brought the lights up. "Fact is, I figure that Inspector Volto incident was rigged by the competition."

"Our client, Maybelle Vexford," Jolson said. "Why's she want the brain found?"

"Just before Starpirate entered the clinic he signed a fat contract for his autobio. Advance is two million trudollars. Mrs. Vexford gets forty percent of that for ghosting the darn book."

"That's an incentive, sure enough. How'd she contact BIDS?"

"Went to a branch office on Esmeralda," replied Molly. "After the prelims were taken care of, she was put in touch with me by way of sat/pixphone."

"Did you ladies mention me during your chat?"

Molly looked down at her folded hands. "Well, she mentioned to me that an ex-Chameleon agent might be a good idea and I . . . well, I assured her she could have our best ex-Chameleon. That's you, Ben."

"Why's she think a shapechanger is called for?"

"I don't have all the details, but she hinted she may have a lead on the thieves," said Molly. "My impression is they're an unsavory bunch, and our BIDS operative is going to have to venture into some seamy spots on Esmeralda and mingle with a lot of vicious and mean-minded lowlifes."

"Another typical case."

"I'd really like you to take this on, but—in view of the fact somebody tried to bump you off before you even got going—I'll understand if you decline."

Grinning, he stood studying her pretty face for a few quiet seconds. "Is this a new Molly I'm experiencing? Usually you holler and threaten me with Devil's Island Twenty-five if I don't agree to accept—"

"Devil's Island Twenty-six is where they stick contract violators."

"I'll take the job," he said. "Since the agreement I signed with you and your father seems to obligate me to keep working for BIDS—well, I might as well work on interesting cases."

She hesitated, then smiled. "That's fine, because, you know, you really are the best."

He agreed with her appraisal with a quick nod. "I'd better get out to Esmeralda as soon as—"

"I've booked you on a spaceliner lifting off at eight this evening," she informed him. "Oh, but you'd better not go as Ben Jolson, since somebody seems to know what we're up to. You'll have to assume a new iden—"

"I'll take care of that," he assured her.

"You'll travel out there as somebody else entirely?"

"Yep."

She took a deep breath. Leaning, she kissed him on the cheek. "Don't get killed, please."

"Glad you reminded me of that," he said. "No, I won't."

CHAPTER 4

Jolson folded his warty green hands over his ample midsection. "Heck and shucks, missymam, them is right nice words to hear," he drawled, a broad smile appearing on his toadman face. "In my humble way I try to do the good Lord's work, and if I can touch the hearts of a few million sinful souls by the way of my simple little *Wambam Hour of Electronic Fingerpoppin' Prayer,* why, doggone my britches, I sure now figger I'm on the right enough road and headed for glory."

The little old birdlady who was standing beside his table in the upper-class passengers' saloon on the spaceliner S.S. *Fleetfoot* made a pleased, sighing sound through her cracked yellow beak. "I have to tell you, sir, that Buckminster and I—Buckminster's my dear husband; that's he over at the bar there kidding good-naturedly with that four-breasted barmaid—Bucky and I just never miss a FaithNet vidcast of the Reverend Willy Dee Showcase."

"Oh, that there fills me with joy." Jolson chuckled.

The real and true Reverend Showcase was, according to Jolson's researches, crusading in a remote part of the universe. Therefore it was relatively safe for Jolson, using the abilities he'd acquired as a onetime agent of the elite Chameleon Corps, to turn himself into an exact simulacrum of the video evangelist. This new identity ought to protect Jolson from attacks by crazed andies and anyone else dedicated to keeping him from hunting for Starpirate's brain.

"This should help, Reverend." The birdwoman dipped a claw into her plazpurse, extracted a twenty-trudollar note and held it out toward him.

"Well, bless you all to heck, dear lady," he said. "But whatever is it for?"

"The good work you're engaged in on the planet Murdstone." The orange-and-blue piece of money fluttered in her grasp. "Bucky and I have already contributed to the building of the Reverend Willy Dee Showcase College for Religious Commandos and the Reverend Willy Dee Showcase Palatial Mansion Fund, and now we surely wish to help you and your darling little wife, Curly Mae, build the Reverend Willy Dee Showcase School of Devotional Tap Dancing."

"Oh, missymam, I am deeply touched. May Saint Serpentine and Saint Reptillicus both shine their blessings down on your sweet feathery head, and on Bucky as well."

"Amen."

"Oh, amen indeed."

"Dear me, Captain Berdanier seems to be criticizing my husband about something," noticed the birdwoman. "I'd best trot over and intervene. Bless you, Reverend."

"Same to you, dear lady." Reaching, he plucked the twenty trubux from her and tucked it into a pocket of his lemon-yellow waistcoat.

Over at the long ebony bar the captain of the Esmeralda-bound spaceliner, a portly catman in a three-piece white sparklesuit, was gently pushing a gaunt old birdman back away from the vicinity of the blue-skinned barmaid. She was pulling up the shoulder strap of her glodress.

Jolson drummed his stubby green fingers on the table, turned to gaze out at the awesome blackness of space beyond the clear viewindow.

"Don't be a goon," said a somewhat familiar female voice a few tables behind him. "Do a scramola."

Turning, he saw a slim young woman with rainbow hair glaring up at a gorillaman who was leaning over her table and resting his gloved paws on it. The girl Jolson had met before during his sojourns for BIDS, and the gorilla was the same one who'd stepped on his foot at the detective equipment show.

"C'mon, sis, be a sport," the gorilla was whispering. "Have a snort with a lonesome space wayfarer."

"Take off, you dunk," she suggested. "I don't fraternize with strangers."

"You better make an exception, baby," advised the whispering gorilla. "I like your looks and—ook!"

Jolson had gone over, taken hold of the collar of the gorilla's pinstripe jacket and tugged him up and away from the table. "Pardon me for butting in, pilgrim," he said, "but I simply can't sit by while a pretty little critter is being annoyed."

"Go spit up a rope," whispered the gorillaman. "This is between the bimbo and me. I don't need no Holy Roller to—unk!"

Smiling beatifically, Jolson had delivered an impressive punch to the gorilla's ribs. The blow caused the man to double up some and clutch at himself. "If you was to spend the rest of the evening in prayer and contemplation, son, I truly do believe you'd benefit."

"Oomph," muttered the gorillaman.

Still smiling, Jolson hurried him across the lounge, into the corridor. He gave him a boot in the backside to hasten his return to his cabin.

When Jolson returned, the young woman with the rainbow hair said, "I know you."

"No doubt you do, little missy." He paused beside her. "For the good Lord has seen his way clear to making me universally famous."

She gave a snorting laugh. "Don't try that crapola on me, Rev," she told him. "I've seen your ratings and, glory be, you don't even pull as big an audience as the Right Reverend Ricky Marshall and His Sanctified Accordion Band." She shrugged her narrow shoulders. "Anyhow, thanks for saving me from the attentions of that boof."

"All part of my duty to my fellow beings, missy."

She was poking her fingers into her small, overstocked purse. "I might as well introduce myself." She lifted a bizcard free of the clutter, handed it to him. "Careful, it tends to overheat."

Jolson knew that and grasped the card gingerly between thumb and forefinger. "Right nice to—"

"INTRODUCING," boomed the voxcard, starting to give off a wispy spiral of bluish smoke, "MISS TIMMY TEMPEST, REPORTER-AT-LARGE FOR *GALACTIC VARIETY!*"

Dropping the smoldering electronic card to the glaz tabletop, he inquired, "What takes you to Esmeralda, little missy?"

"INTRODUCING MISS—"

"Enough already." Timmy sideswiped the smoking card into her purse and shut it away. "Well, heck, what I'm involved with is a fate worse than death. I have to turn out a three-hundred-fifty-word story for *Galactic Variety* on some dunky event known as the Fourth Annual Dopestix Jazz and Folk Musicon. It's a pretty dippy planet that's had three previous Annual Dopestix Jazz and Folk Musicons."

"Might just be, dear child, that the Lord has another reason for you to be journeying to—"

"Sure, maybe I'm destined to do a write-up on you for *Galactic Variety.*"

Jolson smiled. "Heck, now, an article on the many good works I been doing across this old universe'd lift up the hearts of a whole lot of—"

"Nertz. That snerg-and-pony show you put on doesn't even rate fifty words on a back page. But thanks for giving that dunk the heave-ho," she said, rising and starting for the exit. "See you around."

"You probably will," said Jolson forlornly.

CHAPTER 5

The next assassination attempt came roughly two hours ahead of setdown on the planet Esmeralda.

Jolson had awakened a few moments earlier, sat up in his bunk and yawned greenly. He got out of his candy-stripe nightshirt, scratched at his plump pebbly side and went trotting across the soft lavender floor to the bathroom compartment.

"Thanks, Lord, for letting me make it through to another day," he muttered.

Having checked the orange-walled compartment for bugs and other spy devices, Jolson knew no one was eavesdropping. He liked to stay in character anyway.

Once inside the sonicleansing cubicle, he flipped on the appropriate toggles and then commenced singing a hymn having to do with marching in the army of Saint Reptillicus.

He was croaking his way through the second verse when a tiny gadget he was wearing attached to his left ear made a tiny buzzing.

That meant somebody had tripped the alarm by coming into his cabin parlor.

Stepping free of the shower stall, he grabbed up a stungun he'd left atop the crimson toilet earlier. He placed himself with his back to the blue wall near the doorway. Someone stepping into the bath compartment wouldn't immediately spot him.

He'd left the sonic nozzles on and kept singing while he was repositioning himself. Now, coming to the end of a verse, he ceased his warbling.

About half a minute after that the door slid open. A uniformed catman leaped across the yellow threshold, his stungun aimed at the humming stall.

"Wellsir and doggone," remarked Jolson, "if it ain't the captain his own self. Morning to ya."

Captain Berdanier took two surprised steps into the small room. He started to swing his furry head and his silvery gun around toward Jolson.

"Just you make like a doggone statue, Cap," advised Jolson, prodding the catman in the back with the barrel of his stungun.

"Ah, there, Reverend Showcase, I fear there's been a mistake on my part," said the captain in an uneasy voice. "Yes, I find myself in the wrong pew entirely. You may well imagine my chagrin."

"Not a nice idea to come leaping into anybody's biffy toting a weapon," he said. "What I'd be mighty pleased to have you do is drop that pretty gun of yours on the floor and give it a nice kick."

"Really, Reverend, this whole—"

"You just do it, Cap, and mighty quick." He jabbed the gun harder into the furry back.

"Perhaps it'll clear the air, yes." Grunting, the portly ship's officer bent and dropped the stungun onto a purple plaz throw rug. He tapped at it with his boot, causing both rug and gun to slide over against the stall door.

"Nothing like a few deep bends to limber a fella up of a morning," observed Jolson. "You mosey on out into my parlor."

"This is actually simply a—"

"Sit yourself in that pretty polka-dot slingchair."

The captain obliged, scowling at Jolson, whiskers erect. "If you wish to get dressed, I'll gladly step into the corridor until—"

"Shucks, the good Lord knows what all my equipment looks like, and I ain't worried about nobody else's opinion." Sitting on the edge of the bunk, he gestured at the catman with his stungun. "Why'd you drop in on me so sneaky like?"

"As I've been trying to explain, Reverend, I mistook your cabin for that of . . . well, of a lady who was anxious to have a . . . well, rendezvous and—"

"Here I been working my toke off to improve the moral fiber of the universe and danged if there ain't as many liars around as they was when I commenced." He left the bunk, keeping eyes and gun on the captain. From the small suitcase at the foot of the bunk he took a pale green disc. "Let's have us an honest chat, Cappy."

"See here, I much resent your—oof!"

Jolson had slapped the truthdisc against the catman's furry neck and it took hold. "You'll answer all my questions truthfully."

"Yes, I will," droned the now mind-controlled captain.

"Why the visit?"

"I was ordered."

"To do what?"

"Stun you first, then administer a shot from the medigun I have in my pocket," Captain Berdanier replied. "The injection would induce all the symptoms of a fatal heart seizure, a perfectly natural death."

"Why'd anyone want to bump off honest godfearing Reverend Showcase?"

"You aren't Showcase."

"Oh, so? Who am I, then?"

"Ben Jolson, a shapechanging operative with the Briggs Interplanetary Detective Service."

Jolson cocked his head. "How do you know that?"

"BIDS booked this cabin, for one thing."

"But through a cover agency."

"The cover's name is known. Therefore, whoever took this cabin would be an ex-Chameleon."

"Who put you up to this?"

The furry-faced captain answered, "The Whispering Gorilla."

"Him again. Who is he?"

"A criminal."

"Yep, that I figured out on my own. Who's he work for?"

"He is, among other things, the collection agent for several gambling casinos in the Barnum System. Casinos that I owe considerable money to."

"That's how they persuaded you to take a try at murdering me?"

"They offered to cancel a hundred thousand trudollars off my debt."

"Not much of a price for me," reflected Jolson. "Hell, I ought to be worth two or three times that. Who's the Whispering Gorilla's boss on this one?"

"A man known only as Professor Tincan."

"A cyborg with a metal head. I've heard of him, yeah. Rumored to be a member in good standing of the Galactic Mafia," said Jolson. "Why do these two gents want me defunct?"

"To keep you from finding Starpirate's brain."

"How do they know that's what I'm after?"

"I have no idea."

"Do they know where the thing is hidden?"

"I have no idea."

"Where's our soft-spoken gorilla now?"

"He left the liner half an hour ago aboard the Express-Mail shuttle for Esmeralda."

Jolson returned to the bunk. "Tell you what, Captain. You'll wake up in a half hour and you'll forget this entire conversation," he told the brain-controlled catman. "When the Whispering Gorilla gets around to asking you how things went, you tell him everything went along as planned. I passed on to glory, it was accepted as a natural death and the body shipped home to Barnum. Maybe that'll stall them for a bit."

"I shall do as you say, sir."

"Thanks." Jolson retrieved his truthdisc.

The furry captain went to sleep.

CHAPTER 6

By the time Jolson reached the outskirts of the capital city of Jazinto Territory it was early afternoon and his feathers were drooping in the hazy heat. He'd ditched the skycab he'd hired at the spaceport ten miles ago and come the rest of the way through the hot yellow streets on foot.

The light breeze that was blowing through the narrowing streets was warm, dry. It rubbed at the glaring white, yellow and red fronts of the low brix buildings, worried the steep-slanting neotile roofs. The brittle fronds of the high, thin palm trees rattled quietly. Most of the small shops and stores were locked and shuttered. Signs reading *Nap* could be seen in many of the windows.

Breathing in and out through his yellow beak, Jolson slowed and scanned the dusty afternoon street. In a hammock slung between two sudowood columns in front of a wineshop a heavyset frogman slumbered.

Jolson walked on by the snoring vintner, turned uphill at the next corner.

Hill after hill, each thick with jungle foliage, rose away

beyond the city. There was a hazy green glow to everything up there.

Swinging his neowicker suitcase with only a minimum of verve, Jolson began climbing a broad pathway that cut up through the green brush and trees. Scarlet-and-emerald parrots were perched on the crosshatch of branches, making shrieky small talk. Huge golden butterflies flickered in and out between shadow and sunlight.

Eventually he came to a fork in the wide trail. On his left, nailed lopsidedly to the bole of a squat yellowish tree, was an arrow-shaped sign: *Bananas, Inc. Budd Timmons, Pres. & Chairman of Board. Banana Tastings Every Tues. & Thurs.*

"Shame it's Wednesday," remarked Jolson, taking the left-hand road.

The dogman guard at the wide-open gate of the many-acred banana plantation was sleeping soundly in a rubberoid slingchair, his stunrifle sprawled across his knees, his tongue dangling out of the side of his open mouth.

Jolson eased by him without upsetting his slumber. He walked along a blue gravel path until he reached a large, rambling neowood house.

Sitting on the veranda in a tin rocker was a plump, balding man of about Jolson's age. He was wide awake, a stungun dangling in his left hand. "Buckminster deMollay, is it?" the man asked.

"How'd you figure that, Budd?"

Timmons replied, "I keep well informed, even in the sticks. The spaceport law found his unconscious form and that of his missus in their upper-class passengers' cabin aboard the freshly arrived S.S. *Fleetfoot.* Buckminster deMollay, birdman, passport and disembark permit missing. Rated thirty seconds on the NewsNet channel, between a commercial for Dopestix and a report on grout rustling over in the next territory." He rocked a couple of times in his chair. "Don't suppose you're in the mood for a wedge of banana cream pie, Ben?"

Jolson considered. "Perhaps later."

"Stungunned poor old Bucky and his spouse, did you?"

"Very mildly, yep." He sat on the railing facing Timmons. "Didn't have much choice. They dropped in on me just after I was forced to put the captain of the damn liner into a stupor. I needed a new identity to sneak off the ship, and there was Bucky. I forgot how hot feathers can be."

Timmons said, "I haven't done a birdman—or any other alternate ID, for that matter—since I retired from the Chameleon Corps four years ago. 'Twas my notion that you'd said good-bye to all that too and were now occupied in honest toil. Or as near as you can get to honest toil in the ceramics trade. Then you all at once pix me—using a portable scramblebox no less—and announce you're on my home planet working on a case and would like to use my humble plantation as a hideaway for a spell."

"I figure this'll be safer than the hotel."

Timmons rubbed at his chin. "Do you like banana strudel?"

"I could learn to. This case I'm working on is—"

"Pretty face, exemplary figure."

"Hum?"

"Molly Briggs," said Jolson's erstwhile colleague. "I can understand how you were persuaded to join the BIDS outfit."

Jolson said, "Soon as it was learned I was heading out here, people started trying to arrange my demise."

Timmons rose up, slowly and carefully, a few of his joints creaking and complaining. "C'mon inside and we can talk this whole business over," he said. "I'm about to fix up lunch. How do you feel about bananaburgers?"

"Open-minded."

"Oh, and since I know what you actually look like, you can cease portraying dear old Bucky."

Jolson did that.

Timmons finished eating his banana, rubbed his fingertips along the seams of his checkered trousers, pushed back from the portable dining table he'd set up in his parlor. "Sure you don't want another bowl of banana soup, Ben?"

"I've had sufficient, thanks." Jolson was himself again, wearing his own clothes.

"You've adjusted pretty well to being an ex-Chameleon."

Jolson gave him a sideways grin. "My idea of adjusting would be to quit the impersonations completely and—"

"Nope, you can't really do that." Timmons leaned an elbow on the table. "Once you've been processed you never lose the urge to assume other identities. Now and then, at least."

"Don't think I have that particular urge."

"But you do, Ben. Working for this interplanetary detective outfit, though, gives you a way to satisfy the urge," Timmons explained. "Me, I lack such an outlet. Sometimes—and don't tell anyone this—I still do a shape-change. When I'm, you know, all alone here."

"Nothing wrong with that."

The second elbow rested on the tabletop. "You were always better at certain things than I was, back when we were both crackerjack Chameleon Corps agents dashing around the universe in the service of truth and justice," he said. "Since I retired, however, I've been practicing. For instance, you were always ahead of me at doing inanimate objects. I still remember that time we snuck into the embassy on the second moon of Murdstone and both had to pose as refrigerators. You were much more believable than I was—I even forgot the ice-cube trays." Timmons chuckled at the recollection. "One time on that satellite bordello orbiting one of the Hellquad planets you spent three days as a love seat in the—"

"What say we return to the present and make my pix-call to—"

"You never did women, though, did you?"

Jolson shook his head. "That tends to unsettle me."

"That's because of hidden doubts about your core identity." Timmons left the table, moved to the tin chair that faced his pixphone. "A coin-operated therapist in a spaceport on Jupiter told me that once. I was always the same way about working in drag, but some of the CC ops thrive on it." He smoothed a wrinkle out of his trousers. "Just thought of another thing you were better at. You could always elongate your arm, send your hand snaking clear across a room or out a—"

"Like this?" Jolson was still at the table, but he'd stretched his arm out until his right hand was resting on the dial panel of the pixphone. After punching out a number, he contracted his arm to its normal length.

A strikingly beautiful blonde android appeared on the

phone screen, smiling enthusiastically. "Tell me how the Interplan Pixphone Company can be of service, madam."

"Sir," corrected Timmons. "Okay, I want to place—"

"Goodness, I'm dreadfully sorry," apologized the golden-haired mechanism, blushing and bonking her temple with the heel of her hand. "My RecogSyst is due for its two-thousand-hour tune-up and hence—"

"Understood. Now I want to make a sat/pixphone call to the planet Barnum. To the private residence of Molly Briggs. Her numb—"

"Does your mommy know you're playing with the phone?"

"Give yourself another whap on the coco, honey."

The lovely android blushed once more. "Forgive me, sir," she said, shaking her head violently from side to side for a few seconds. "There, that ought to fix it. I'm perceiving you as a bald, middle-aged man on the obese side. Is that correct?"

"Close enough." He gave her Molly's number. "Hasten."

"All IPC calls are put through swiftly, sir. Something that cannot be said for our many second-rate competitors across the universe. While your call is being speedily processed you'll be entertained with an interesting and informative travelog entitled *The Best Swamps on Murdstone.*"

Slumping some in his chair, Timmons glanced over at the pacing Jolson. "Should you ever decide to give up this sleuthing business, I'd be delighted to take you in as a part—"

"Hello?"

Molly, red hair wrapped in a towel, was frowning out

of the pixphone screen. She wore a striped shirt and green slacks.

"Hi, MB," said Timmons. "I've got import—"

"Budd Timmons? You've gone to seed since quitting CC, but I still recognize . . . Wait now. You live on Esmeralda. Has something happened to Ben Jolson? Is that—"

"He's extant," the plump ex-Chameleon assured her. "Before we continue this jolly discourse, Moll, you have to do a couple things."

"I don't quite under—"

"Is your antitap gadget on and functioning?"

"Well, certainly. I just paid twenty-six thousand trudollars for the latest, and best, on the market, so naturally I'm going to—"

"Splendid and admirable. Next go over your domicile to make certain nobody's planted a bug on you of late."

"We have the whole place checked once a—"

"Moll, do it."

"Is Ben there? Ben, is all this silly. . . . Oh, all right. Hold on a sec."

"Very attractive lady," observed Budd.

"I've noticed," said Jolson, moving up behind his friend's chair.

"This is sort of odd," said Molly when she returned to the picture screen. "There was a bug, a little dinky one, hooked under a coffee table. Esmeralda manufacture."

"Just one?"

She nodded. "Yes, I made certain."

"Then here's your star employee." Timmons started to rise, then sat again. "By the way, MB, if you ever want to buy bananas at discount, let—"

"Molly," said Jolson, hefting his former colleague out of the chair and taking his place.

She sighed, laughing. "You're not dead," she said. "That's a relief. Off-planet calls always scare me, because most often they're bad news or—"

"Listen, there was another try at doing away with me." He gave her the details.

"The captain himself? Darn, they aren't going to get away with that," Molly said, angry. "I'll demand a refund on your passage and—"

"As a result of all this attention being paid to me," Jolson cut in, "I'm not going to be residing at the hotel you booked for me. You can contact me here at Budd's plantation until I get a safe place to use as a base."

"Yes, that's best," agreed Molly. Frowning, she tangled her forefinger in her auburn hair. "Who exactly is behind these murder attempts?"

Jolson leaned forward. "There's a lot more competition for Starpirate's brain than we knew about going in," he told her. "The Whispering Gorilla works for a gent called Professor Tincan. Thus far they seem to be the only ones who're openly anxious to get me off the trail. However, according to what Budd's been hearing locally, the Political Espionage Office—probably on orders from its central headquarters on Barnum—has a couple of agents hunting that brainchip. Supposedly they're interested in the political material, the Saticoy memoirs and such. Several political cronies of the dumped dictator are also eager to find out what Starpirate did with the Saticoy archives. It's also highly possible that some of Jackland Boggs's buccaneer buddies are interested in his missing brain. They, as might be expected, want to know where the loot is hidden. It's likely I'll be bumping into various and sundry agents who—"

"Ben, I better come out there to Esmeralda."

"Nope."

"You haven't given me a chance to mention all the new crimefighting equipment I ended up buying when I went back to that show," she said. "I'm very good at backing you up, and with all this new stuff I can—"

"You remain on Barnum," he said. "At least until I find out more about whom we're competing with. It isn't exactly safe for you here right at the—"

"If I was that crazy about safety, Ben, I wouldn't have become a private eye in the first—"

"Stay right there. I'll contact you again tomorrow," he promised and cut off the call.

Timmons started peeling himself another banana. "That's the sort of job I sometimes yearn for," he said. "Where the boss's lovely daughter is head over heels in love with—"

"Go tend to your bananas," suggested Jolson.

CHAPTER 7

The heavy night rain slammed at the skycar and the harsh wind caused it to bounce and weave as Jolson flew toward the villa that was his destination. The cabin leaked some, and the heating unit was on the fritz and spewing out purplish mist.

The skycar was the worst in Timmons's fleet of six, but it was the only one that didn't have *Bananas, Inc.* lettered on its sides and underbelly in throbbing glolet-ters.

Jolson was still himself, having decided that was the best persona to use in calling on their client.

Spotting the multidomed hillside villa of Maybelle Vex-ford, he punched out a landing pattern.

Swaying, making irregularly spaced gulping sounds, the borrowed skycar lurched down through the dark and rain. It barely missed scraping its underside on the top of the high glazbrix wall, then dropped close to the ground, clipped some branches off a few of the decorative trees and thunked to a landing on the gravel area near the sprawling glaz house.

Jolson sat for a few seconds, listening to the rain pattering on the metallic roof. He sighed once, undid his safety gear and stepped free of the skyvehicle.

He ran through the rain to the porch area of the main dome. Five feet from the doorway, he slowed. The doorway was open, the door apparently jammed.

"Mrs. Vexford?" he called from the threshold.

The visitor vidscan camera over the door moved a few ticks to the left, eyed him.

The sound of falling rain hitting on the domes of the villa echoed through the place.

"Mrs. Vexford?"

Someone moaned, very faintly, inside.

He eased out his stungun from his shoulder holster, took a few careful steps into the dark hall.

There was a cluster of glowing light balls floating high in the giant living room to the right. On the silvery thermocarpeting were three bodies.

A butlerbot, the top of his coppery head sliced away by a lazgun, was flat on his back near the wide arched doorway.

Further into the room a pretty maid android, face down, lay with wires and shards of glaz spilled out of the jagged hole in her side.

Near the fireplace the birdwoman author he'd come to see was sitting wide-legged on the floor, her broad back resting against the side of a Lucite armchair.

Jolson ran across to her, knelt. "Mrs. Vexford, I'm Ben Jolson from BIDS."

Her tiny dark eyes were glazing over. Both claws were clutched to her bosom, but they were unable to stop the blood spilling out of the two kilgun wounds.

She muttered, "I . . . thought he was . . . I thought he . . . was Dr. Chow . . . Chow . . ."

"Dr. Chowderman? Was he—"

"But . . . it wasn't he . . ."

Jolson glanced around, located the pixphone alcove. "I'll phone for—"

"Listen, Jolson," gasped the author through her orange beak. "About Starpirate's brain . . . find . . . you have to . . . find Balooka . . . he . . . knows where . . . Balooka . . . The Islands . . ."

That was all she'd ever say. Her eyes snapped shut, her claws forgot what they were doing and she died.

"Damn." Jolson stood up.

He scrutinized the room. On the carpeting near the dead birdwoman was the faint outline of a large, damp bootprint.

Jolson carefully made his way back to the doorway, noticing three other prints. "Could be the tread of the guest she thought was Dr. Chowderman."

The small screen of the vidscan camera he found mounted in the plaz wall to the left of the front door. Right now it was showing a view of the rainswept front porch.

From his trouser pocket Jolson fetched an electropik. He removed a panel of the vidset, poked around a bit and persuaded the mechanism to allow him to reverse and fast-forward the vidtapes it had made in the past couple of hours.

Besides himself there had been no visitors except a stocky greatcoated catman who looked a hell of a lot like the electrosurgeon who'd performed the brain transfer on Starpirate.

"Except she said it wasn't actually Chowderman at—"

"Hey, I'm going to enjoy this." A wide man was coming in out of the rain, his metal right hand pointing at Jolson. "You remember me, don't you, Ben?"

"Sergeant Hillman of the Territorial Police Murder Squad, sure."

"Lieutenant now," the thickset cyborg corrected. "Things change, Ben, as the years pass. You, for example, aren't a Chameleon Corps agent anymore. That means the Political Espionage Office doesn't cover your ass anymore."

"Instead of chatting about old times, suppose you go into the living room," he said. "There's a—"

"Hey, I know what's in there, Ben," said the cop. "Respected old bird bimbo, knocked off by you. We got a pixcall to that effect."

"C'mon, you know damn well I—"

"Remember my hand?" Hillman jabbed his metal forefinger into Jolson's side.

A sharp shock went jerking through his body. Jolson bit down on air, his head snapped far to the right, he stumbled, fell against the wall.

"Added all sorts of new gimmicks since last we met, Ben," said Lieutenant Hillman, smiling, watching Jolson gasp for air. "I think, maybe you don't recall, the prod finger is much stronger now. Feels like it, doesn't it?"

"Hillman," said Jolson, his voice thin and weak, "don't try to—"

"Fellas, toss this suspect in the skyvan."

Two botcops, taller and wider than Hillman and with black enameled bodies, rolled in. Each one grabbed an arm and they escorted Jolson out of the dead author's villa.

When Jolson opened his eyes, he saw first the grey ceiling of his cell. Next there came into his ken the smiling face of a silver-plated android in a two-piece green bizsuit.

"This looks very good for our case," said the android in his deep, impressive voice. "We've been collecting very impressive settlements lately on these police-brutality things. Just stay sprawled there a moment longer while we catalog all your bruises, contusions, hematomas and—"

"Who," inquired Jolson as, causing himself considerable pain, he got up off the grey floor of the small grey cell, "the hell would you be?"

"Your attorney." From a slot in his silvery left hand popped a business card. "Newne and Hickey's the name. Actually, Newne and Hickey Two Hundred Thirty-six. We—"

"Newne and Hickey? That cheesy franchised lawyer operation that dispenses law the way other people sell soyburgers? Who hired—"

"Your benefactor was lucky to get us," the mechanical lawyer informed him. "Not many firms want to handle a case such as yours, open-and-shut murder and rape with—"

"Hillman isn't claiming I assaulted that old lady as well as bumping her off?"

"The Territorial Police are charging you simply with slaughtering Mrs. Vexford in cold blood," replied Newne and Hickey. "The sexual assaults involves the maid, a very expensive imported android named Fifi. Under Esmeraldan law, which is based in part on the universally accepted laws of robotics, anyone forcing his or her attentions on a mechanism is treated as though—"

"Okay, fine." Jolson made his way to the grey cot, sat. "How soon can you get me out of—"

The android attorney chuckled. "That's the spirit. We like to see a client with a sense of humor. You won't get out of here, Mr. Johnson, until—"

"Jolson."

"Really? Are you certain? Well, yes, we suppose you'd know. The point is, Mr. Jolson, that when you've committed a series of brutal crimes the bail situation is . . . Did we mention you'll also be charged with sodomy?"

"With the butler?"

"Yes, exactly. Well, since you seem to be ready to face the responsibility for the crimes you've committed, we may be able—"

"I haven't committed any crimes. Which Hillman damn well knows," he told the andy. "All he has to do is play the vidtape and he'll see that Dr. Chowder—"

"Dr. Chowderman—a respected member of the community, by the way—has an airtight, ironclad and foolproof alibi for the time of the killing."

"Nevertheless, he's on that tape in all his furry—"

"The police contend it's you who is to be seen on that tape, Mr. Jolson—did we get it right that time? You see, Mr. Jolson, for a defrocked Chameleon Corps agent such as yourself it would be a piece of cake to assume the identity of a respected—"

"And then I come back later as myself to—"

"You returned, according to the police, to erase the scanner tape."

"What'd I do with the weapons I used?"

"Disposed of them when you took off the first time."

Jolson nodded slowly. "Who hired you?"

"Why, you hired us," replied Newne and Hickey. "Or at least the person who did said he was acting on your instructions."

"You saw this benefactor?"

"Actually, no. The phonescreen remained black. That often happens in cases where—"

"How were you paid?"

"Cash, teleported to our offices."

Jolson asked, "When do I go up before a judge?"

"We'll find that out." The attorney moved to the narrow grey door. "If you'll excuse us, we have several other criminals to visit while we're here."

Jolson made a dismissing gesture. "Keep in touch," he said.

CHAPTER 8

"You got to eat something for breakfast, pal," urged the trustybot. "You don't want to starve to death before your execution."

"I haven't even had a hearing in the two days I've been here," Jolson pointed out from his reclining position on his grey cot. "So discussing my execution is a bit prem—"

"You want I should recite the menu to you again?" asked the ball-headed coppery robot.

"It'll pass the time."

"Okay, you got a choice of gruel, gruel with nuts and berries, gruel with fiber, gruel with dates and raisins, gruel with bananas, gruel with snergbits, gruel with—"

"Make mine with bananas."

"Coming right up, pal." The bot punched a button on his coppery chest, held his other hand out over the plaz bowl on the cell's small grey table. Porridge came spewing out of his thumb.

Sitting up, Jolson said, "I haven't heard from Newne and Hickey since my first night—"

"That's a pretty rinky-dink law firm." The robot shook

his thumb and a last dollop of brownish mush fell free. "You'll be lucky if you see that guy again before—"

The cell door suddenly whooshed wide open.

A handsome gold-plated android, wearing a glistening three-piece tuxsuit, came bounding in. "Let's go, Jolson."

"Hm?"

"Perhaps we need a few formalities first, eh? To be sure." The gleaming android smiled, flashing diamond-studded silver teeth. "My card." From the breast pocket of his shimmering ebony jacket he drew a talking business card.

"INTRODUCING MR. POWERS THUNDERBALL, ATTORNEY-AT-LAW," announced the card in a deep, handsome voice. "HE'S THE BEST. 'NUFF SAID."

"Geeze, the highest-priced shyster on the whole blooming planet," murmured the trusty, edging toward a corner.

Jolson stood. "You mentioned getting me out of here?"

Dropping his card away with a swooping flourish, the gold-plated attorney produced a packet of legal forms, documents and notes. "You're free as a snerg," explained Thunderball, diamond eyes flashing. "We can depart."

"What about all the charges against me?"

"Dropped." Reaching out, the attorney took hold of Jolson's sleeve and tugged him toward the wide-open doorway of the cell. "Come along now."

Jolson complied. "Who got you to—"

"Hey, pal," called the trustybot, "you want I should

wrap up your gruel so as you can take it along? Meals may be few and far between on the out—"

"I'll forgo that." As he and the attorney walked rapidly along the grey corridor he asked, "What happened to Newne and Hickey?"

"Replaced by me."

"Okay, and who hired you to take the case?"

"All that will be explained."

They started down a ramp with a glaz doorway at its end. The outside world showed through the panels. "Explained by who?"

"A skycab awaits you without," Thunderball told him. "The autopilot has been instructed to fly you to the party or parties who paid my fee. That is all I'm at liberty to divulge at—"

"Hey, Ben."

Jolson halted, turned and looked up the ramp. "I was hoping I'd get a chance to wish you farewell, Hillman." He took a few steps in the direction of the approaching policeman.

The android grabbed at Jolson's sleeve again. "No brawling, no frumus of any sort."

Hillman laughed. "Ben's not going to take a sock at me, Counselor. He knows better than that."

"Eventually," Jolson said evenly, "we're going to encounter each other someplace where you don't have—"

"I'll always have my hand." He held it up, smiling. "Hey, I only wanted to remind you you're not out of the woods yet, Ben. Don't leave the planet just yet."

"Didn't intend to."

"We have a schedule to maintain. Good morning, Lieutenant." Thunderball got Jolson moving again.

He allowed himself to be escorted out of the Murder Squad jail and into the chill early-morning air.

"We are now passing over the main factory of Dopestix," said the automatic skycab. "As you may not know, this particular cigaret was invented right here on Esmeralda and went on to become popular throughout the universe. Dopestix are not habit-forming, not dangerous to your—"

"About our destination?" Jolson, alone now, was slouched in the passenger seat of the aircraft, ignoring the unfolding view of the morning city.

"We'll be arriving there in a few shakes, sir," said the voxbox on the dash. "Gaze down to my right and you'll see the famous Territorial Museum of Stuffed Dragons, one of the wonders of—"

"How long is a few shakes in minutes?"

"Four and a half, sir."

Nodding, Jolson slouched further.

Five and a half minutes later the skycab settled down to a landing in a clearing in the woods beyond the capital.

Jolson bid his cab a quick farewell and disembarked.

"Get in touch with me any time you want to see the sights." The orange vehicle rose up and flew off in the direction of the city.

Across the small clearing, surrounded by a garden rich with bright blossoming flowers, stood a neowood cottage. It had a tilting brix chimney, a slanting sudothatch roof and stained-glaz windows. Roosting on the eaves were three plump pink pigeons.

The door of the cottage came swinging slowly open. Jolson moved his right hand to his shoulder holster.

Sniffer trotted out into the pale sunlight. "Don't just stand there with your ugly puss hanging out, boneyard," spoke the robot dog. "Truck on inside here."

CHAPTER 9

Jolson pocketed his bug detector, came back into the cozy parlor. "Okay, there aren't any spy devices in—"

"Didn't I already attest to that, dimwit?" Sniffer was spread out on a candystripe love seat, one bright metal paw dangling over the edge. "When I run a security sweep of a joint, you can bet your—"

"Did you buy him outright or are you just renting?" Jolson asked Molly.

The redhead was sitting in a neowood rocker near the small brix fireplace, one long bare leg tucked under her. "Before we get down to chatting, Ben, I really would like to see you fellows make up and—"

"I'm not going to negotiate with a machine, especially one that wags his tail."

"Molly, you don't even need this nurf any longer," said Sniffer. "With me on the job, BIDS'll forge ahead like—"

"Snif, you're forgetting what I told you on the way out here from—"

"Just because you've got the hots for this beanpole," cut

in the robot dog, "is no reason to jeopardize the handling of a major case. Ship him back on the next spacetug aimed at Barnum and allow me to—"

"That's enough." Molly shook her head at Sniffer, nose wrinkling. "You be still and polite, or I'll ship *you* home in a crate."

Jolson asked her, "How'd you know I was in jail?"

"Budd Timmons pixed me," she answered. "And I hired an attorney powerful enough to spring you and get all the charges tossed out. Are you sure you don't want to see a doctor? You have bruises and lumps all over your—"

"A chintzy play for sympathy," Sniffer pointed out, scratching a metal ear with a paw. "Any ex-Chameleon could obviously get rid of those with—"

"Another lawyer came to see me," Jolson said. "Name of Newne and Hickey. I'd like to find out who hired—"

"Preston Zuck hired that bucket of bolts," said Sniffer. "I found that out while we were still coming through customs at the spaceport. See, I've got some terrific built-in info-tapping stuff in my—"

"Who's Zuck?" he asked Molly.

"He's Maybelle Vexford's literary agent, a rather effete man who—"

"Guy's a roaring fruitcake," said the robot dog, rolling his plaz eyes.

"Mr. Zuck is now our client," said Molly. "He feels it will honor Mrs. Vexford's memory if the bio of Starpirate is written anyway and—"

"That old nance smells moolah," observed Sniffer. "He'll hire some pitiful hack—which most free-lance writers are—to take over. Pay 'im a niggardly flat fee, reap huge profits and—"

"Hush up," Molly advised him. "Mr. Zuck is a bit on the conservative side when it comes to money, Ben. It took some doing to get him to agree to our BIDS fee. When he heard you'd been arrested, he decided to hire an attorney to help you. But, being Mr. Zuck, he went for the inexpensive—"

"Maybe you ought to consider dumping the whole case," said Jolson.

"Typical Jolson strategy," said the dog. "Turn tail, to use a canine metaphor, and run."

"Our original client got killed," said Jolson. "Somebody tried to frame me for the job. Now if this guy Zuck isn't even going to pay us top money, we—"

"As a matter of fact," said Molly, "he finally agreed to give us a substantial bonus if we find the missing brain. I pointed out to him that the quest has terrific publicity possibilities for promoting the book and—"

"We don't want any publicity right now. There are enough folks who know I'm—"

"I'm not completely dippy. He won't send out a single PR release until you bring in the brainchip and get safely back," Molly told him. "And you don't have to act as though I'm going to futz up your investigation, Ben. Keep in mind that I came out to this darn planet in the first place just to get you sprung from jail. Had I not paid Powers Thunderball a fat fee—he charges a minimum of eighteen hundred trudollars an hour—to get you free of that place, you'd still be rotting in—"

"All right, okay. I'm deeply grateful." Jolson started pacing the parlor. "If we're going to stay involved in this, then we have to find out several things before we continue."

"That's exactly why I brought Sniffer and some other new equipment along with—"

"I saw somebody who looked quite a lot like Dr. Chowderman on our late client's visitor tape," Jolson said, walking slowly across the flowered carpet. "The real doctor supposedly has an alibi. I want to make sure of that before—"

"Already did that while you were guzzling down jailhouse gruel," the robot dog informed him. "Dr. Albert J. Chowderman was nowhere near that skwack's abode on the evening of the crime."

"You can take his word for that, Ben. Snif's chock-full of the very latest data-gathering and info-tapping gadg—"

Jolson said, "Okay, if it wasn't the real and true Chowderman, then we're probably dealing with a shapechanger. Meaning either the Political Espionage Office has assigned a Chameleon Corps agent to the hunt for Boggs's brain or there's an ex-Chameleon working on this for somebody."

Molly said, "Snif's done some digging there, too."

Without looking at the chrome-plated hound, Jolson asked, "What did he find out?"

"The PEO office on Barnum contacted the Esmeralda field office here in the capital five days ago," said Sniffer. "The locals have assigned an agent named Hunz Hungerford to head up the search for Starpirate's missing brain. PEO is allegedly interested only in the Saticoy political material."

"Is Hungerford working with a CC agent?"

"Nope."

Jolson decided to sit on the flowered sofa. "That means one of our opponents is using an ex-Chameleon, an ex-Chameleon who can be hired to murder folks."

"Shining morals ain't one of the qualifications for a CC career," Sniffer pointed out.

"Ben, we have a list of the only three former Chameleon Corps agents in this part of the planet," Molly said. "There are others, a few anyway, elsewhere on Esmeralda, but we can start with these three."

"Evelyn Milman," said Sniffer, "Wally Trumbower and Budd Timmons."

Shaking his head, Jolson said, "Budd's in the banana business and nothing else. Also happens to be a friend of mine who—"

"He's four hundred twenty-six thousand trubux in debt even as we speak, chum."

"Can you link him to any of this?"

"Not yet, but I'm—"

"Forget him, then."

"Fellas," said Molly, "quit glaring at each other. We're supposed to be a team."

Standing, Jolson said, "Maybelle Vexford told me, as she was expiring, to look for somebody named Balooka."

"Yes, that'd be Rudy Balooka," said Molly. "He was one of Starpirate's crew, although they haven't been very close for the past couple of years."

"He's a birdman, who'd have to spruce up some to be classed as scum," added Sniffer. "Known to have tried to visit Boggs at Dr. Chowderman's establishment."

Jolson said, "He could've swiped the brainchip."

"One of Balooka's specialties is safecracking, Ben."

"Mrs. Vexford also mentioned The Islands," said Jolson. "That's a space colony orbiting this planet, as I recall, gotten up to look like an archipelago of tropical paradises inside."

"Used to be just that," said Sniffer. "In recent years it's fallen in stature some. The Islands is shunned by tourists and vacationers these days, but much loved as a hideout by crooks, cutthroats, scoundrels and other dregs of the uni. You'll fit right in, slim."

"Sounds like a place Balooka might hole up at."

"And a place you'd have to use a new identity to infiltrate," said Molly. "Mrs. Vexford, poor soul, did hint that she had some idea about who might've made off with the brain and that chasing after him would involve hitting some dangerous places." She shifted, put both feet on the floor, rested her palms on her bare knees. "Snif and I'll need some sort of disguises too, to accompany you when—"

"Whoa," said Jolson. "I'll visit The Islands solo. You can—"

"Listen to this bag of bones," commented Sniffer. "Send the gink on a simple visit to a client and he ends up letting her get bumped off. Thereafter he allows the local flatfeet to hustle him into the hoosegow. Molly, you need some new blood in this outfit. I can scoot up to The Islands, track Balooka to his lair, retrieve the piratical brainchip and—"

"Sniffer," she said, a bit impatiently, "I'm in charge of this operation. Be still now or I'll have to put you away in the closet again."

Jolson grinned. "Good place for—"

"You weren't going to blab about that," said Sniffer, miffed.

Molly got up and crossed to Jolson. "Okay, go to The Islands alone," she said. "We'll stay here and keep digging for background stuff. If there's any trouble, holler." She kissed him on the cheek.

Putting his paws over his plaz eyes and groaning, Sniffer said, "Such mush."

CHAPTER 10

Jolson, walking a shuffling walk, left the ramshackle shuttle and made his way across the creaking disembark ramp and into the woebegone metal docking area of the space colony. Scabs of bright orange rust dotted the rutted walkways and the dented walls. Busted crates and spilled produce containers were scattered about, and furtive, fuzzy little rodents frolicked amidst the debris. The whole passageway smelled of decay and animal droppings.

"Well, you've made another mistake, Father," said the chubby catwoman who was following in Jolson's slightly zigzag wake on the shaggy arm of her chubby catman husband.

"Nonsense, Mother, this is only the entryway to The Islands. A preamble as it were to—"

"I just stepped in rodent doody, Father."

Increasing his shambling pace some, Jolson moved further ahead of the scatter of passengers who'd shared the bumpy shuttle ride up here to The Islands.

At the twisting corridor's end stood a partially ajar metal door, with a sign that read *The management of The*

Islands accepts absolutely no responsibility for ANYTHING that happens to you during your stay herein. We are not responsible for your rape, moral collapse, degradation, murder or anything else. The sign had had sundry other comments added to it over the years. There were lewd and derisive comments scrawled in glopaint, throbink, electropencil and what looked to be blood. The languages of several planetary systems were in evidence, and it seemed no one had a good word to say about this orbiting satellite.

Jolson pushed the door a bit further open, stepped inside and took a few jerking steps. He was on what appeared to be a stretch of sandy beach. A few yards downhill was a foamy surf and then an expanse of blue sea dotted with small tropical islands. Pale yellow gulls glided through the blue of the perennially afternoon sky.

A neowood staircase angled down through the bright tangle of green, orange and yellow brush that grew up beyond the beach. Jolson trudged across the warm white sand and started up the weathered steps.

Above the brush, some five hundred feet above the sea, was a wide dusty street. Two blocks long, it consisted of eleven saloons and bars, three run-down hotels and a large burned-out ruin that was still fronted with a glosign declaring it was the Main Island Shopping Mall. Although a few people, human and otherwise, roamed the sun-drenched street, most of the denizens could be seen, or at least heard, in the various bistros.

"Hey," called a gruff voice from behind him, "what the hell are you trying to pull?"

Jolson halted on the swayback neowood sidewalk he'd

been shambling along. "Was you hollering at me, pal?" he inquired, turning around.

"Damn right I was." Standing under the battered bamboo awning of the saloon Jolson had just passed was a large thickset lizardman in the garb of a sailor.

"Well, what do you want, pal?"

The lizardman scowled, tongue darting angrily in and out of his mouth, as he came closer. "I know you," he said, pointing a large green forefinger.

Jolson leaned casually back against the trunk of a sidewalk palm tree. "So what?"

"So how come you're high-hatting me, Charley?"

Jolson was not himself. Decked out in a rumpled, dirt-smeared white suit and neopanama hat, he had assumed the persona of a human known as Jakewalk Charley. The true and original Charley was languishing in a prison satellite two planet systems away. Jolson was gambling that what few friends and associates Charley had on Esmeralda wouldn't be particularly aware of his present whereabouts.

He squinted at the green sailor, scratched at the grey stubble on his negligible chin. "I'll tell you, pal, I been in stir again," he explained in his thin, whining voice. "The bulls give me some therapy—stuck my coco in a brainbox a few times." He tapped his temple with a shaky hand. "Made me a little forgetful, you know."

"Hell, then let me introduce myself all over again, Charley." He held out his scaly right hand. "Dornford Yates, second mate of the *Scarlet Queen.*"

"Pleased to meet you, Dorny." He shook hands, then made a few anxious shuffling movements. "Now I got to see some guys at Bob the Beachcomber's. Things been rough and maybe I got me a job in the—"

"Listen, Charley." Yates leaned nearer, eyed him anxiously. "The screws didn't reform you, did they?"

Jolson laughed a whining, nasal laugh. "Fat chance."

"See, because Jackazee is around town right now and he—"

"Who the hell is Jackazee?"

"Holy cow, they really did futz up your bean," observed the lizardman. "I'm alluding to Swifty Jackazee, the goddamn president of the Esmeralda Chapter of the SCU."

"Oh, yeah, the Slavers Corporation of the Universe."

Yates sighed. "Good, you ain't forgot everything." He rested a hand on Jolson's shoulder, further rumpling the dingy white suit. "Jackazee is interested in picking up some . . . um . . . merchandise, if you get my drift."

"Naw, I don't want to mess with the skin trade. A nice simple heist, or a smuggling job, is okay. But I'm not kidnapping broads for intergalactic pimps to peddle to—"

"Hey, Jackazee assures me he ain't after hookers this trip. I wouldn't mess with that either, Charley, since my religious scruples—"

"Since when have you had scruples of any kind?"

"No, listen. I've been watching a really great man on the vidwall, and he's showed me the way to salvation. His name is the Reverend Willy Dee Showcase," explained Yates, glancing up at the palm fronds overhead. "The best thing about his kind of religion is you don't have to give up making a fast buck. Just so long as you send Showcase sufficient donations and abide by a few simple dietary laws, why—"

"I ain't interested in religion or hookers."

"I'm trying to tell you that Jackazee's only after chorus girls for a lavish musical to be staged for the guys who work the skymines out beyond the Hellquad planets. He'll pay a thousand trubux per girl. Twenty percent bonus if she happens to be a virgin."

"I never met a chorus girl who was." Pulling free of the seaman, Jolson turned away. "Let's have a drink sometime."

He modified his shuffle enough to let him increase his pace. He was anxious to get to the meeting that Budd Timmons had helped set up.

What with the breeze generated by the three decorative fans overhead and the gusts of icy air chuffing out of the air-conditioning outlets, the interior of Bob the Beachcomber's was a chill contrast to the warm street.

Just over the threshold Jolson gave an involuntary shiver as he glanced around. There were two dozen neowood tables crowded onto the neowood planking, booths on the left and right walls. Potted palms filled in much of the space between the tables, and the walls were decorated with rattan matting and twists of multicolored fishnet. Each and every table was occupied. A quartet of frogmen in spotless white suits was sharing a plazflagon of skullpop at the nearest table. Sailors, drifters and other lowlifes were drinking, bickering, conniving at the other tables and in most of the neowood booths. The bartender was a huge bleached-blond apeman with a nearsighted parrot perched on his bare shoulder.

Shivering yet again, Jolson took a few steps across the noisy room in the direction of the bar.

"It's sad, isn't it?"

Jolson noticed a large toadwoman in a brightly colored flowered shift sitting on a stool near the swinging doors.

"Hell, I guess if a bozo wants to dye his fur, he—"

"I meant about poor Bob, Charley." The toadwoman extracted a lace-trimmed plyochief from the bosom of her frock and sniffled into it. "Forgive me for mentioning it at all, but I couldn't help noting the way you shuddered when you entered and realized poor Bob was gone."

"Yeah, it did sort of hit me."

"You didn't even know he was sick, did you? Because it's been—how long is it anyway since you were in The Islands, Charley?"

After considering the question, he replied, "Seems like a hell of a long while. What was wrong with Bob anyhow?"

She blew her nose before answering. "The poor guy had Bimrose's disease."

"Sounds rough, although I ain't exactly sure what that particular malady is."

"Well, it's quite similar to Winship's syndrome, except your eyebrows don't fall out."

Shaking his head sympathetically, Jolson said, "Well, I got to—"

"At first they thought it was just Reisbersonitis and the doctor prescribed alfalfa injections." She was crying now, tears streaking her green cheeks. "But it turned out the physician on the case—a cut-rate military medibot from a surplus warehouse on Murdstone—had a defective gudgeon and thought everybody was suffering from Reisbersonitis. The damn bot also had a deal with a pharmaceutical firm that had a large surplus of alfalfa extract, so he was advising just about all his patients to—"

"Ain't it the truth," said Jolson, edging away from the mourning widow. He'd spotted his contact in one of the booths along the far wall.

The thin man in the shadowy booth was covered with tattoos, intricate works of art in green, red and black, each surrounded with a frame etched in golden ink. "Excuse my looks," he apologized as Jolson slid in opposite him. "I've been on a sort of drastic diet lately—at the urging of one of the ladies I live with."

"It does contract your decorations some."

"Here I am, known far and wide as Gallery Jones," complained Gallery Jones, "yet fully half the pictures enhancing my body look as though somebody tried to crumple them up. I mean to say, take a gander at *The Orphan Child Lost in the Storm* here on my chest. The little lass looks like a crone because of the wrinkles in my—"

"I'd like to get to business." Jolson was unobtrusively passing his hand-held bug detector over the tabletop and walls.

"Believe me, Jolson, there are no spy devices in this joint," Gallery Jones assured him. "I already swept the area."

"Even so." He spent another two minutes making sure there wasn't any gadget listening in on them.

"I sort of figured you'd want to chat about my paintings first, seeing as how you're an artist yourself," said Gallery Jones, rubbing his palm across the tattoo of a dying warrior that adorned his wrinkled forehead.

"At the moment I'm a BIDS operative." Jolson rested his elbows on the table. "According to Budd Timmons, you're a reliable source of information about The Islands."

Gallery Jones tugged up his tunic to scratch at his illuminated left side. "Ever since I shed so much poundage, I find *Maiden Bathing at a Forest Pool* itches like the dickens all the time," he explained. "Sure, I'm a former Political Espionage Office agent. Nobody can brief you on this place better than I."

"Why'd you leave the PEO?"

"A woman," he replied a shade ruefully. "A very gifted tattoo artist, but that's another story. What do you want to know?"

"I want to locate Rudy Balooka."

New wrinkles appeared across the dying warrior. "That's getting to be a popular activity."

"Meaning?"

"I hear the PEO's interested in him, and so are certain important politicians on Esmeralda."

"Do they have agents here on The Islands?"

"Not yet, far as I know. You're the first to track Balooka here, but others could start arriving soon."

"He is here, then?"

Gallery Jones nodded. "I can get you his exact location by dinnertime," he promised. "The price is five thousand trubux."

"Nope, it's one thousand."

"Four thousand."

"Two thousand."

"Three thousand."

"Sold," said Jolson.

"Where are you staying?"

"Hotel Stacpoole."

"Best of the lot, which isn't saying much," Gallery Jones observed. "I'll contact you there by eight, set up another meeting someplace."

Nodding, Jolson eased free of the booth.

Just short of the door the mournful toadwoman said, "You missed the memorial service for poor Bob, Charley."

"That I did," he agreed.

CHAPTER 11

The Night Zone lay on the north side of the island, where it was always dark and foggy. Jolson, hands deep in the trouser pockets of his bedraggled white suit, went shuffling along a misty, quirky lane at nine o'clock. The fog was rolling in off the black ocean, drifting through the narrow dockside streets and alleys. A foghorn croaked off someplace unseen, phantom planking creaked, invisible chains rattled.

"Hi, chum. Help a veteran of the war?" Half a man was sitting in a homemade wheelchair at the lane's end.

"Which war?"

"Name your favorite. I fought in a lot of them."

Jolson dropped a buxcoin into the man's plazcup and continued on his shambling way.

Slippery trustone steps led down to the dim-lit entryway to Pegleg Floyd's Waterfront Café. Jolson descended carefully, avoiding the drunken dogman sailor snoring in the damp stairwell.

Music and raw yellow light hit at him as he stepped into the small, low-ceilinged room where he was scheduled to meet Gallery Jones. A naked silver robot was pounding the keys of an upright piano. The mechanical man's dented body was scribbled and scrawled with a multicolored assortment of inscriptions, and he wore a licorice-hued glaz derby at a rakish angle.

"Sweet patootie is the only thing I crave," he bellowed. "Sweet patootie gonna lead me to my grave."

In a small clear space near the short neowood bar two fat apemen in drag were jitterbugging enthusiastically. A midget toadman in a sarong was doing an abandoned hootchie-cootchie dance atop the bar itself. When he stepped barefooted into the open-face sandwich of a piebald catman stevedore, the big dockwalloper plucked him up by the scruff of his pea-green neck and flipped him, unlooking, over his shoulder. The little toad, tiny feet still churning, landed smack on his backside in the center of a table being shared by three conspiring gorillamen. The largest of the three snarled, adjusted his yacht club blazer and took hold of the new arrival by his throat.

"Easy now, easy," called the bartender, a large one-legged catman in a yellow-and-crimson sarong. "We'll have no throttling of the clientele, gov." Puffing some, he stepped out from behind his counter.

"Sorry, Peg," apologized the gorilla as he let the groggy toad midget drop to the sawdusted floor. "My violent temper got the best of me once again, I fear."

"Happens to all of us, Ezekial, and— Well, bless Bess! It's Jakewalk Charley." Grinning, Pegleg Floyd came stumping around the crowded tables toward Jolson. "I thought you were still in the sneezer out on Zegundo."

"Time off," explained Jolson, taking the proprietor's furry hand and shaking it, "for good behavior."

Pegleg Floyd chuckled. "Still the ribber," he said, winking. "Come on into my office, Charley, and we'll—"

"Maybe later, Peg. I got to meet a guy."

The catman nodded, tugging up the front of his sarong. "What you got to do, Charley, is learn to relax," he advised. "Too much business causes stress, and that can lead to such serious diseases as Reisbersonitis and . . . Excuse me a mo. Hey, over there. No suggestive dancing in here, okay?" He went off in the direction of the jitterbuggers.

An illustrated hand caught hold of Jolson's arm. "Over here, I've got us a table," said Gallery Jones. "By the way, why'd you pick a fellow so well known to impersonate? Seems like everybody up here wants to shake your mitt and buy you—"

"Long as they think I'm Charley and not me, it's okay." He followed a weaving path among the tables in the smoky little room.

Two hefty gatormen were asleep at the table Gallery Jones stopped beside. "Heft the other one, will you?" he requested, tugging one of the unconscious sailors clear of his chair and tossing him aside.

After clearing his chair, Jolson sat. "Your fee was deposited in your Banx account on Esmeralda at—"

"Six twenty-seven," said the illustrated man. "I know, I checked up. BIDS is damn efficient."

"Most times," said Jolson. "So tell me where . . ."

A sudden and absolute hush filled the place. The illuminated robot ceased his playing; the apes quit dancing; all the patrons stopped babbling and conspiring; even the little toadman, who'd been moaning near the spittoon, shut up.

The cause of this abrupt silence was the advent of two

new customers. The first was a broad-shouldered lionman in a pinstripe glosuit. Following behind him, walking in careful mincing steps, was a hugely fat toadman in a candystripe robe and scarlet fez. The pair of them came to a stop beside a table near the door. The four large stevedores occupying it shot to their feet, slurped down what was left of their drinks and went double-timing out into the misty night. The fat toad seated himself daintily, patted at his perspiring face with a pink sinsilk hanky and sighed. After glancing around, the lionman sat opposite him.

Slowly, cautiously, the other patrons of Pegleg Floyd's began breathing again, moving, talking.

"The bodyguard's Spooner, the big toad is Swifty Jackazee," informed Gallery Jones in a low voice. "A very powerful gent in—"

"Yeah, I've heard of him." Jolson hunched slightly. "Where can I find Balooka?"

"There's a small island called Laguna Azul," answered Gallery Jones, new wrinkles crisscrossing the dying warrior tattooed on his forehead. "Balooka's holed up there in a rented villa." Reaching across the table, he tapped Jolson's arm. "You may have even more competition than we thought."

"Who else?"

"I've been picking up rumors that an impressively nasty lady space pirate named Flame Flenniken is due here shortly—fact is, she may be here even as we speak."

"A onetime associate of Jackland Boggs."

"That's her. Worked with Starpirate until they had a falling out over loot," said the tattooed man. "She's after Balooka, too, so—oops!" He bumped backwards in his chair, gazing up beyond Jolson.

Turning, Jolson observed that the lionman was looming behind him. "Evening, Spooner," he said before returning his attention to Gallery Jones.

"The boss," announced Spooner quietly, "wants to talk to you, Jakewalk Charley."

"Sure, soon as I finish up—"

"No, he wishes to speak now," explained the big lionman. "Say good-bye to your friend, Jakewalk Charley."

Gallery Jones nodded rapidly. "Good idea. Good-bye, Charley." He was on his feet, scurrying for the door, before he finished speaking.

"Hell, Spooner, you're futzing up my leisure-time activities."

"The boss wants to talk to you, Jakewalk Charley."

Ducking free of the lionman's grasp, Jolson rose to his feet. "I guess I'll go talk to your boss."

CHAPTER 12

Jolson sneezed again. "Nix, Mr. Jackazee," he said, rubbing his dirty knuckles under his nose. "If it's all the same to you, I ain't interested in no—"

"Whatever is the matter with you, dear Charley?" The obese toadman was reclining on a striped divan in the back of his landvan. "Why, you used to adore, absolutely adore, this perfume of mine, and now it really seems to make you just horribly sneezy."

"Aw, it ain't so much the perfume. I just think I maybe got a touch of Reisbersonitis or could be—"

"Well, don't you dare come any closer, then." The large divan bounced as the landvan rattled through the dark, fogbound streets of the Night Zone.

Hunched on a hassock, Jolson whined, "See, it ain't that I ain't grateful for this opportunity, Mr. Jackazee. It ain't that at all. But, see, I got me another job lined up which'll—"

"This little bitsy chore," said Jackazee, toying with the tassel of his fez while he eyed Jolson, "is dreadfully simple, Charley. Gracious, you've done jobs like this for me just dozens and dozens of times before."

"Sure, and I'll probably do them again. The thing is, this time—"

"Allow me to explain the situation more fully." Grunting, huffing, he managed to shift himself to a sitting position. "The young lady in question is—"

"Your skimmer, Mr. Jackazee."

"Eh?"

Jolson pointed. "Your lid, it's about to topple off your noggin."

"Ah, ah, so it is." The president of the Esmeralda branch of the Slavers Corporation of the Universe adjusted his fez. "This young lady happens to be residing at the Hotel Russell here in the Night Zone under the name of Janie Mae Petersburg—a dreadfully unmelodious name, to my way of thinking. In reality, she is Jody Pearl." He paused, watching Jolson.

"Never heard of the bimbo under neither monicker."

Both Jackazee and the divan quivered when he sighed. "Have you never eaten at one of those horribly ubiquitous Eatz fast-food restaurants?"

"I guess, sure. But what . . . Oh, I get it." He snapped his stubby fingers. "This quiff is *that* Jody Pearl—her old man owns the whole blinking Eatz setup. Got franchised spots on forty-six different planets, seventy-two planetoids, ninety-six asteroids, one hundred and eight—"

"I refer to that selfsame runaway heiress, yes, I do." When he rubbed his large hands together, it produced a slippery squeaking noise. "It will amuse me to sell this skinny little blonde wench to the chorus line of *The Skyminers' Vanities.*"

"Wouldn't it pay off even better to sell her pop her whereabouts so as he—"

"Charley, Charley. Am I a common informer?" He spread green fingers out across his broad breast. "Nay, I am a businessman, and the product I sell is women. Three thousand."

"Huh?"

"I'll pay you three thousand trudollars—a frightfully larger sum than you've ever earned with me heretofore—to slip into the lass's hostelry, put her to sleep and deliver her to my warehouse dockside."

"See, the problem is, Mr. Jackazee, I'm in the middle of negotiating—"

"I'd be dreadfully unsettled should I have to instruct Spooner to break some more of your bones," added the huge toadman. "You must still recall what he did to your left arm on Barnum."

"Couldn't we at least wait until—"

"Unfortunately not, Charley dear. I'm on a terribly tight schedule and must have my quota of young ladies—one dozen in all—at the warehouse no later than tomorrow evening. From there Spooner and I shall smuggle them off The Islands in my own private shuttle. By the by, I've redecorated my bedchamber in peach and—"

"Suppose I round up another guy to—"

"Ah, but I want *you.*"

Jolson slumped a bit. "When do you want this damn job done?"

"This evening, the sooner the better." From within his striped robe he brought an ebony gazgun. "Use this on the dear young thing."

Jolson reached out, accepted the gun. "Okay, all right," he said. "I'll get her for you."

"To make horribly certain that all goes well," said the

toadman, smiling broadly, "I'm sending Spooner along with you."

With ease the large lionman boosted Jolson to the top of the high stone wall. "Can you see it, Jakewalk Charley?"

Stretching out flat atop the wall, Jolson gazed across the dark, weedy courtyard at the rear of the three-story, tile-roofed Hotel Russell. "Which window again?"

"Second floor, furthest left."

"Yep, her lights are on."

"Okay, then you scoot up the fire ladder and fetch her."

Easing the gazgun out of his coat pocket, Jolson said, "Lean in closer, there's something important I got to ask you."

"What is it, Jakewalk Charley?"

Pointing the weapon at the lionman's snout, Jolson squeezed the trigger.

Hhhhiiizzzzzzzzzzz!

"You double-crossing . . ." Spooner's eyelids drooped shut, he executed a small stumbling dance, swatted three times at the small greenish cloud swirling around his head and fell to the wet cobblestones of the alley. He remained there, unconscious.

It was at this point that Jolson made a mistake. To avoid having Spooner and Jackazee do violence to him, he'd pretended to go along with this plan to abduct the runaway Eatz heiress. Now that he'd put Spooner out of the way for a while, he could depart the Night Zone and arrange to transport himself to Laguna Azul island.

"But Jackazee'll probably keep trying to snatch the girl," he reminded himself.

That wasn't actually his problem. She'd run off from her happy home, so she had to be prepared for a few rough times.

"Being sold to a pack of loutish skyminers, though . . ."

He let out a breath, inhaled. He dropped from the wall to the dark courtyard.

"Somebody has to warn her. Shouldn't take that long."

Pushing through the overgrown shrubs and knee-high grass, he abandoned the features of Jakewalk Charley and became himself again.

"That'll probably scare her less."

Quietly he jumped, catching hold of the lowest rung of the fire ladder. He pulled himself up, climbed to the second-floor window and took a careful look into the room that was supposed to hold Jody Pearl.

There was a young woman inside. Blonde, slender, pretty and not more than nineteen. She matched the tri-op photos Jackazee had displayed to him in the landvan.

Jody was seated cross-legged on her narrow spoolbed, dressed in dark slacks and a pale blue singlet. She had a plazcarton labeled *Eatz* on her lap and was dipping into it with a plaz fork.

Stowing his gazgun, Jolson tapped softly on the window with his forefinger.

Jody's head jerked back, and she gasped.

He tapped again.

Setting the carton aside, she left her bed and took three tentative steps in the direction of the window, squinting. "What exactly is it that you want? And listen, if you're somebody I know excuse what may seem like rudeness at, you know, not maybe recognizing you right off. I can't wear regular eyelenses because they make my eyes water and get all sort of pinkish and so I have to use the old-fashioned glasses with big ugly frames, except I don't think those help my looks at all and so I'm always taking them off, except then I never, you know, remember where I set the things. Which is exactly what I just did, even though I'm dining alone, if you can call wolfing down this gunk dining. So that's why I—"

"Miss Pearl, if you'll open the window, I'd—"

"Doggone." Jody blinked, shook her head, scratched at her short blond hair. "Here I thought I was safely traveling incognito and unrecognized, and then some Peeping Tom shinnies up the side of my tacky hotel out of the blue to inform me that he knows who I really am. Although, excuse me if I'm insulting you, you may not, you know, be a voyeur or anything, but maybe something really sleazy like an investigative reporter for some sheet like the *Galactic Enquirer* or—"

"Hold it." Jolson yanked out his lokpik, applied it to the window mechanism, opened the window himself and entered her room. "I'm running way behind schedule tonight," he explained, stepping on her threadbare carpet. "But I did want to warn you that you're in some danger, Miss Pearl."

"That suit, if you don't mind my pointing it out, actually doesn't fit you at all well," she said, studying him with narrowed eyes. "What I mean is, you know, you're not that unpersonable as far as looks go, although myself I don't get stimulated much by older men, which you probably don't consider yourself, but you have to remember I'm much younger than you. The suit, to get back to that, is much too tight for one thing, and then, you know, I don't think anybody should wear a white suit in this sort of milieu at all. Even if it weren't unpressed and all wrinkled and a bit smelly, your suit's also stained with mud, rust, cheap wine and—well, I'm not even sure what that green splotch there is, but you probably know better than I, so—"

"Attend to me," he requested, more than a shade impatiently. He started to speak, paused to sneeze. Her perfume, though different, was nearly as strong as Jackazee's. "Some rather disreputable gents have learned who you really are. They figure to kidnap you, sell you into slavery. Myself, I've got other things to attend to, but I did feel I ought to at least warn you in order—"

"Wow, boy! My father just doesn't give up, huh?" She laughed. "Tracks me to this out-of-the-way spot, which no less than three separate travel agents assured me was more remote than the most unheard-of boonie planet, has his agents find me and then sends some seedy out-of-work actor, which is what I guess you must be to go along with a dippy plot like this, to come stumbling into my hideaway with a silly scare story that's so ancient it wouldn't frighten a—"

The neowood door of her room all at once ceased to be there. It had been turned to dust by a brand-new Dorammer pistol. The pistol was in the furry hand of Spooner. "You sure are turning out not to be very reliable, Jakewalk Charley," he said, stepping across the threshold. "You coldcock me and . . . and, say, you even went and changed your face."

Jody came over to take hold of Jolson's left arm. "I think maybe I'm commencing to believe you," she admitted.

CHAPTER 13

Jolson did several things at once.

He shoved the blonde young woman aside with his left hand, causing her to go stumbling toward the bed and topple over atop it. The abandoned Eatz carton leaped high, scattering neorice and soyballs.

Jolson dived to the right, tugging out his stungun. Hitting the floor, he rolled over twice and then fired up at the intruding Spooner.

Zzzzzuuuuummmmmmmmmm!

The lionman had been swinging his pistol around to aim at the moving target that was the white-suited Jolson. The beam of the stunner took Spooner in the chest and he stiffened, arms flapping out at his sides. He managed to pull the trigger on the Dorammer, but missed Jolson entirely and disintegrated the room's only chair.

Backwards he fell, landing flat in the shadowy hall.

Jody was kneeling on the bed, squinting in the direction of the fallen intruder. "Is he some personal enemy of yours, because he did, you know, make what sort of sounded like a nasty remark about you after he blasted away the door, or is he one of those fellows you mentioned who're intent on abducting me for—"

"Both." Jolson stepped into the hall, retrieved Spooner's pistol from where it had fallen. "If you can pack rapidly, I'll escort you to—"

"Actually I never really much unpacked." She swung off the spoolbed. "And I only brought one dinky suitcase when I took off from our mansion on the planet Murdstone, which is one of seven mansions we have, or maybe it's eight because I do think my father just bought another one. I had it in mind to travel light. Probably you haven't ever given it much thought, although perhaps you have, since, when you come right down to it, I barely know you, but when one's making a getaway one really doesn't want to haul a whole stewpot of trunks, valises, reticules—"

"Gather whatever it is you've got." Bending, he took the stunned lionman by the armpits and dragged him into the room. "I'll take you to the shuttle dock before I go on about—"

"How many, would you guess, other slavers and thugs are out there with designs on me?"

Depositing Spooner beside the bed, Jolson answered, "One, at least."

"Mightn't he, you know, have minions?"

"More than likely."

Jody hurried to the closet, avoiding the spilled contents of the food carton, and took out a small sinleather suitcase. "Don't, now, get the notion I'm cowardly or, like some of these spoiled multibillionaire heiresses you've heard about, that I have an exaggerated notion of my importance," she said. "The thing is, though, I think I'd feel definitely uneasy waiting around for the next shuttle to depart. What's to stop these slavers from making another try for me in that docking area? They don't, at least they didn't when I landed here two days ago, have any guards on duty around there or even a single run-down old copbot to protect—"

"I don't have time to hang around there until—"

"Well, what I'm getting at is, how long are you planning to stick around The Islands? What I mean is, I could tag along with you, you know, and I'm not, although sometimes I talk a little too much if I'm excited or have met someone I find truly interesting, a nuisance and I promise not to get in your—"

"No," he said. "Nope."

"Actually I'm not exactly certain what kind of work it is you do," she said as he took hold of her arm and guided her to the doorless doorway. "I've been, in the midst of dodging kidnap attempts and watching you cleverly outfox the threat, trying to figure out what sort of job would require the ability to shinny up the sides of old tacky hotels and the wearing of unfashionable suits with really crummy stains all over the front of them. Apparently you also go in for disguises, since I assume that's what the slaver was alluding to when he charged in here and mentioned that you'd altered your—"

"We'll try the front way out of this hotel," he said quietly. "From now until we get down to the street you are to maintain a discreet and total silence." He pulled her along the corridor with him.

"Well, I can certainly keep quiet," Jody assured him. "It's not as though, you know, I'm some kind of compulsive babbler, even though my Aunt Irene surely is and I suppose you could make out a valid case for that sort of thing being hereditary, except for the fact that she's only my aunt by marriage and, anyway, Uncle Si was married six times, at least, before Aunt Irene came into the picture, so there isn't even the chance of an environmental infl—"

"Hush," he advised.

Jolson, alone and still himself, made his way along the sunlit dock. He'd changed into one of his own outfits, a three-piece tan cazsuit.

Sitting in front of a shack of an office, directly under a weathered glosign that read *Skipper Jellicoe: Boats Rented for All Occasions,* was a middle-sized rabbitman in a conservative three-piece grey bizsuit.

"Is the Skipper around?" inquired Jolson.

"I am he." The rabbitman's whiskers wiggled as he stood up and held out a paw. "Welcome aboard, matey."

Shaking hands, Jolson said, "I want to rent a launch."

"Um," said Jellicoe, glancing over the dock edge at the half-dozen seacraft moored in the water just below his business shack. "A launch, is it? Um . . . sure, swab. We must have one of those."

"That crimson-and-gold launch ought to do." Jolson pointed. "How much?"

"Is that a launch?" The Skipper's nose wrinkled, his pinkish eyes widened. "Now, avast ye, had I but known that yesterday I'd have earned a pretty penny. But I've been going along thinking it was a yawl."

"Like to rent it for a day or two."

"You seem to be knowledgeable about the sea, lubber. Could I prevail upon you to inform me which one of those boats down there *is* a yawl?"

"You don't have a yawl."

"I don't? How about a ketch?"

"Nope."

Nodding a bit forlornly, Skipper Jellicoe wandered into his shack. "Would you mind stepping into my office for a moment?"

Jolson followed him into the one-windowed neowood room, stepping carefully to avoid the piles of letters, memos and back-issue faxzines sprawled on the plank floor amidst the scatter of ropes, life preservers, fishnets and small anchors. "Is there a deposit or—"

"Just let me make a few corrections in my catalog, then we can settle down to business." He sat behind a small desk that was heaped with papers and nautical paraphernalia. "Shiver me timbers, but it's a blow to find I don't own a ketch or a yawl."

"What's out there is two launches and four seacruisers."

"Blow me down." Jellicoe sighed. "It's starting to look as though I've been bilked and hornswoggled."

"You just bought this setup?"

"Been at it exactly five weeks, ever since I retired from my job as a galactic public accountant and came here to The Islands in search of romance and adventure on the bounding main." He located his price list and began making corrections. "I don't suppose you noticed a galleon out there either?"

"Not a one."

Leaning back in his chair, the rabbitman said, "I've got a rather dashing captain's cap and a burly pea jacket on order, but now I rather think— Ahoy! Who's that?" He half rose, staring at the window.

Jolson spun, hand sliding under his jacket toward his shoulder holster. "Damn," he commented, recognizing the face at the window and letting go his stungun.

"Are you going to be, you know, awfully annoyed with me?" asked Jody Pearl when she appeared in the doorway, her lone suitcase held up against her chest like a shield. "Up to a point I'm impressively courageous, yet when you abandoned me at that forlorn shuttle dock, I was overcome with all sorts of fears and trepid—"

"I'm not going to be able to haul you back there again, so you'd best—"

"Actually I did a rather neat job of tailing you here, and if you weren't so intent on assuming the grouchy exterior you've been led to believe impresses wide-eyed and somewhat madcap little rich girls, you'd admit that I might even be an asset in whatever sort of enterprise it is you're about to engage—"

"Okay, all right. I'll take you along," he said. "But you're going to have to take a vow of silence. And don't come bitching to me if you end up assaulted and maimed."

"That was much more likely to happen at the dingy shuttle dock than it will be wherever you and I are—"

"How much for the launch?" Jolson turned to the Skipper.

The rabbitman smiled and his ears wiggled. "On the house, matey," he said, making an expansive gesture with his right paw. "The business information you've imparted to me is worth more than the price of a yawl . . . oops, of a launch."

CHAPTER 14

The launch moved swiftly across the water, its automatic controls aiming it straight for Laguna Azul island. Jolson sat in the glaz-walled cabin, scanning the dotting of other islands they were passing through.

Jody came in from the deck, cleared her throat and took the other plazchair.

She hummed a little, tapped her fingers on her knee, coughed.

Finally she said, "There are one or two things, you know, that I'm still curious about."

"No doubt."

"For instance, I'd like to address you by your name, except that, and I hope you'll excuse me if it's some old hallowed traditional name that's been in your family for generations and generations, Jakewalk Charley seems like a dippy name to me and I—"

"It was assumed."

Jody smiled, relaxing in the chair. "Well, that's a relief. What I mean is, you know, I don't think I'd feel comfortable calling you either Jakewalk or Charley and certainly not Jakewalk Charley," she admitted.

"Our relationship's going to be short-lived, so it really doesn't much matter what—"

"We're companions at the moment, though, and whenever you address me as Jody, I'd like to be able to reciprocate by—"

"Ben."

"That's your name? Ben?"

He nodded.

She crossed her legs. "Well, I suppose that's a step up, though a small one, from Jakewalk. Ben. Personally, and not meaning to reflect on you as a person in any way, Ben doesn't strike me as much of a name either. To my way of thinking, which is admittedly personal and idiosyncratic, names like Rex and Vernon and—"

"Biffo?"

She frowned at him. "Biffo, no, isn't an especially neat name for a man."

"But you were engaged to a gent with that tag. Biffo Rumhauser," Jolson reminded her. "I remember reading about it in the *Galactic Enquirer.*"

"Oh, them. They tend, as a seemingly bright person such as yourself ought to know, to exaggerate every casual friendship into a torrid romance," she said, shaking her head. "I actually don't think I was engaged to Biffo at all, yet if I was, it couldn't have been for more than a few weeks. I suppose, you know, he must've been a nice boy, but he really didn't make much of an impression on me. Imagine being married to him and having to say, 'Hello there, Biffo,' every time he came into the room."

"Isn't he the lad who gave you the famous Rumhauser Ruby as an engagement present?"

She grew thoughtful. "Well, I suppose he must've been,

since the thing is named after his family. Except that, and don't think I'm bragging about the fact that my father is worth something like six billion trudollars, when you have whole stewpots of fabulous gems of your own, one dinky ruby doesn't always make that much of an—"

"Land ho!" announced the voxbox on the control dash.

Jolson stood to look at the small island they were approaching. Beyond the small lagoon they were entering was a narrow half circle of white beach. Then came a gentle slope rich with foliage. Palm trees, thick ferns, flowering brush, tangles of vines. And there was an absolute quietness about Laguna Azul and no hint that anyone at all was living there.

Pressing down gently on Jody's shoulders, Jolson forced her into a sitting position on a log at the crest of the slope. "Remain right here," he ordered.

"But, you know, I could probably be a good deal of help to you in case you—"

"Since I don't know what I'm going to find at the end of this trail, I want you to stay here where it's safe."

"We don't, actually, know how safe it is even right here on this uncomfortable log perch. What I mean is, there's no telling what's lurking in these woods. Could be all sorts of dangerous cutthroats or—"

"Stay here and remain silent." Turning away, he started off along the narrow pathway that cut through the thick, shadowy jungle that covered most of the small island.

"Well, obviously I'll remain silent, since I'm not the sort of dippy person who sits around and talks to herself. After I've been more or less abandoned in the wilderness, it isn't likely I'd go on prattling and . . ."

The thick green jungle closed in around Jolson, and after that there was a deep quiet. He continued on for several moments, aware of his footfalls and the faint rustling of fronds and branches overhead.

Gradually the jungle started to thin. He slowed his pace, moving more cautiously.

Up ahead was a small clearing with a fairly large villa sitting there all alone. A sprawling place of pinkish sudomarble and slanting blue tile roofs.

From where he squatted at the jungle edge Jolson could see that the front door, up at the top of the wide curving neostone staircase, was gone. Shot away.

He stayed crouched, listening. Then he rose, went running in a zigzag pattern across the bare gritty ground of the clearing and up the stairway. His stungun was in his hand when he reached the gaping doorway.

Nothing came out of the villa. No sound, no indication of movement.

Jolson dived across the threshold, landing on the mosaic tiles of the long corridor that ran clear through the place to another missing door at the back of the villa.

Scattered in the hall were a half-dozen empty Eatz cartons and several pairs of candy-striped socks.

On his right was a large room furnished as a den. It was in disarray. The faxbooks that had once decorated the shelves were now on the thermocarpet, mixing with more discarded Eatz boxes and several mismatched socks. Fallen on its side, metal legs in the air, near the desk was a brainbox.

"Just the thing Balooka'd need to tune in on Starpirate's brainchip," Jolson said to himself.

After another glance around the room, he started for

the door. Something protruding from under an Eatz carton attracted his attention, and he stooped to tug it out and up. A fragment of a map of some kind. Might not be important, but Jolson tucked the two-inch fragment into a side pocket of his jacket.

He'd taken only a few steps along the long corridor when he heard a howl of pain coming from out back.

"Lay off, Flame! Give a bloke a break!"

Sprinting, Jolson ran toward the rectangle of bright sunlight at the other end of the hall. He halted in the doorway and was in time to see a tall, handsome red-haired woman dressed entirely in black—black trousers, black boots, black tunic and black headband—carrying a small, struggling blue-feathered birdman off into the jungle like a sack over her shoulder.

"The lady pirate," Jolson muttered, taking aim with his stungun.

"Ben."

He looked back over his shoulder. "You were supposed to wait back—"

"Sorry, but I'll take over from here." Jody had a stungun of her own. She fired it.

Zzzzzzummmmmmmm!

CHAPTER 15

Outside the lace-curtained window, birds were singing contentedly in the peaceful and serene sunny morning. A warm, gentle breeze softly fluttered the curtains and wafted in the pleasant scent of blossoming flowers.

Jolson lay flat on his back in a four-poster bed, wearing a nightshirt of polka-dot pattern.

After contemplating the pale blue canopy for a moment or so, and wondering what the outdoor birds had to be so aggressively happy about, he sat up.

He felt mildly woozy, his joints seemed to be in need of lubrication and there were some new and unexpected pains in his lower back. Ignoring all that, he got himself out of bed to stand barefooted on a carpet that had interlaced apple blossoms and rosebuds all over it.

He yawned, rubbed at his lower back, took in the room. There was no sign of the clothes he'd been wearing when he'd stupidly, allowed himself to be stungunned by what no doubt had been a spurious Eatz heiress.

"This isn't Laguna Azul," he informed himself, glancing at the pleasant woodland outside the bedroom. "It isn't even The Islands."

There was something a mite familiar about the room. Jolson figured he'd remember where he'd seen it before as soon as his mind turned a bit less fuzzy.

Quietly he walked to the door and tried the handle. It turned and the door opened.

"Well, dimbulb, you finally decided to get off your ox."

This was the parlor of Molly Briggs's rented cottage on Esmeralda. Molly was nowhere to be seen, but Sniffer was lolling on a love seat and eying the emerging ex-Chameleon disdainfully.

"My clothes," he mentioned, taking a few unsteady steps into the larger room.

"I wanted to have them fumigated and then donated to the Home for the Impoverished and Unfashionable," said the robot hound. "Her nibs, alas, hung them in yonder closet."

"And whereabouts is Molly?"

"She ankled out to the nearest forest pool for a morning dip. Very rustic."

Reaching out, Jolson rested a hand on the back of a fat flowered armchair. "You two transported me here from The Islands?"

"Yessir, after finding you flat on your toke in some ragtag villa on a rinky-dink island about the size of a flea's quiffer."

Jolson asked, "How'd you know where I was?"

"The lady of the house got an anonymous tip." Sniffer scratched at his plaz nose with a glittering metallic fore-paw. "My advice was to leave you where you were until you turned to compost, but she insisted on hiring a private shuttle and blasting off to your rescue."

"What kind of anonymous tip?"

"Blank-screen pixphone. Made, as determined by a simple bit of detection on my part, by a gent from a pay phone up in that rumdum satellite." The dog yawned, changed his position on the cushions. "We shlumped to the spot indicated and there you were, looking like a bundle of old laundry. Though nowhere near as appealing."

"How long ago was this?"

"We gathered you up last night, sport, and you've been snoozing in your crib ever since."

Jolson started for the closet.

Sniffer observed, "Judging by that sorrowful expression on your pan, you're still suffering from the aftereffects of your recent bout of stunning. Or were you also hitting the sauce in that piratical hideaway?"

"She had the stungun at its highest setting, apparently. Wanted to make certain I stayed out for a while." He opened the closet, found his suit hanging in among a crowd of Molly's dresses and coats.

"She? I might've known you let a skirt lead you astray," said the dog. "That's the trouble, as I keep striving vainly to convince Moll, with humanoid help. A good mechanism'll never get the hots for some broad, never get snookered into—"

"True," admitted Jolson, reaching into a pocket of his coat and fetching out the scrap of map he'd found in the villa Rudy Balooka had suddenly vacated. "All too true."

"Had I been bloodhounding that second-string space buccaneer, I sure wouldn't have—"

"Ben, you're okay again." Molly came in from the bright morning, wearing a short terrirobe and rubbing with a matching white towel at her long red hair.

"Just about." He crossed to her.

"When we first found you, I really thought you were dead and gone." She put her arms around him, hugging. "But you weren't. I'm very glad of that and . . ." After hesitating a second, she kissed him. Several times.

He said finally, "We have to have a chat."

"Before you do anything further," advised Sniffer from the love seat, "get rid of that nightgown, put on some trousers and hide your spindly pins from the world."

Shaking her head ruefully, Molly said, "I am just a tiny bit disappointed in you, Ben. Letting a featherbrained young woman barely out of her teens lead you up the garden path. I would've thought—"

"That wasn't a young woman just out of her teens." Jolson was slouched on the love seat Sniffer had recently, and reluctantly, abandoned. "Probably wasn't a female at all."

"Whoops, my dear," remarked Sniffer from the fat hassock he was now occupying, batting his metallic eyelids. "Whatever were you up to in that tropical paradise?"

"I should've tumbled earlier, since he slipped up a few times on his background stuff," said Jolson. "I'm pretty certain the Jody Pearl I encountered was actually Wally Trumbower. He was one of the few male agents, when he was serving with the Chameleon Corps, who didn't mind doing female impersonations."

"Bingo," said the robot dog, eyes flashing. "That makes sense, because I've been able to establish beyond a doubt that this Trumbower gink is definitely the ex-Chameleon who's been employed by a group of politicos who're anxious to find the Saticoy material before the government or the media."

Molly tucked one bare leg under her, watching Jolson. "Did you ever become a woman?"

"Nope, I won't work in drag."

She kept on watching him. "When you were fraternizing with that . . . person . . . did you . . . were you . . . intimate?"

Grinning bleakly, he answered, "It was purely avuncular on my part. What I have to do, though, is curb my tendency to help women who appear to be in trouble."

"A dumbbell trait that the forces of evil are full well aware of," the dog pointed out. "That's how they set you up, aware that you simply couldn't pass up a dame in distress. Especially a rich one."

"Yep, it's obvious Jackazee and Spooner were hired to set me up with the imitation Jody," said Jolson. "That way Trumbower could keep track of what I was up to and intervene before I caught up with Balooka."

"But you were passing as Jakewalk Charley," said Molly. "How did they know you were really Ben Jolson?"

"The opposition already knows I'm out here," he answered. "And my informant up in The Islands knew who I really was. More than likely he was paid to inform someone else that I was there and what I was up to."

"In the humble opinion of yours truly," put forth Sniffer, "even *you* didn't know what you were up to. You went stumbling along from island to island, buddying up with double-gaited—"

"That's enough," suggested Molly.

From his jacket pocket Jolson took the map fragment. "Before Balooka got caught up with by Flame Flenniken, he seems to have spent some time tuning in on the information stored in the brainchip," he said, holding up the scrap of multicolored faxpaper. "I figure he found out where the loot—or at least part of the loot—was hidden. He got hold of maps of the area and was scanning them when that lady pirate popped in and swept him off his feet. Soon as we can identify the map this came from, we can get to the area. That's got to be where Flame Flenniken, Balooka and Starpirate's brain have—"

"Let me take a gander at that." The robot dog hopped off the tufted hassock, hit the floor with a bonk and trotted over. Rising up on his hind legs, he snapped the fragment from between Jolson's fingers and swallowed it. "Won't take me long to identify this."

"Next time you plan to swallow evidence, Snif, warn me in advance." Jolson rubbed at his fingertips.

Sniffer announced, "My intricate and admirable internal scanning equipment informs me that what we have here is the lower left-hand corner of Official Esmeralda Map number 104/232G. The map in question shows a ten-square-mile area of the Farmstead Territory, including the benighted town of Triggersville. Retail price of the map is twenty-two trubux."

"Farmstead Territory." Molly placed both feet on the floor. "That ties in, Ben."

"With what?"

She replied, "We've also done some checking on Professor Tincan."

"The gent who employs the Whispering Gorilla?"

Sniffer snorted. "How many criminal masterminds dubbed Professor Tincan do you imagine there are residing on this cheesy planet? Obviously Moll's alluding to—"

"Cut it out," Molly warned the robot dog. "What we've found out, Ben, is that Professor Tincan, the Whispering Gorilla and several of his nastiest stooges are heading for that same area. His cover is a bunch of landvans stuffed with all sorts of gambling equipment. The professor calls the whole shebang the Kasino Karavan."

"Claims he's going to be offering the fun of legalized gambling to the rubes and sodkickers who inhabit that agricultural area," added Sniffer, padding back to the hassock and hopping aboard.

"But most of Farmstead Territory, especially around Triggersville, has been suffering from drought, blight, dwindling income, foreclosures and all sorts of other calamities," continued the red-haired young woman. "The people thereabouts don't have any money to throw away on games of chance."

"Meaning Tincan has other reasons for dropping in on the farm belt," said Jolson.

"It seems likely that somehow he has gotten wind of the fact that some of Starpirate's loot may be hidden there."

Jolson stood. "That's one more reason why I'd better get to Farmstead as soon as I can."

Molly stood. "We'll both go."

"Nope. There's no need for—"

"Ben, I still happen to be your boss—and please don't think I'm trying to throw my weight around—and I am going with you to Farmstead Territory." Hands on hips, she stared at him. "Just because you fell into an obvious trap up in that satellite and let them flimflam and then incapacitate you, Ben, don't think I don't still have faith in your capabilities."

"Snicker, snicker," remarked the dog.

"But this whole darn case is turning out to be a lot more complex than we anticipated," she went on. "We're dealing with murderers, crooked politicians, pirates, female impersonators and gosh knows what else. That means I don't want just a lone operative on it, but a team."

Jolson sucked in his cheek. "Molly, I can handle the whole damn—"

"Darn it, I'm not debating this. I'm just telling you what we're going to do."

After several seconds of silence he said, "Okay."

CHAPTER 16

The jeweled rings on Jolson's furry fingers glittered and gleamed as he lit a kelp stogie. Chuckling and wheezing contentedly, he leaned his bulky catman body back in the comfortable rear seat of the swiftly moving armored landlimo. "Ah, nothing so relaxing as a rural ride and a good smoke," he remarked, blowing yellowish fumes at the sinsilk ceiling.

"Nertz," observed Sniffer, who was disguised as a real dog and sitting uneasily on a folded plaid blanket as far away from Jolson on the landlimo's backseat as he could get.

"Ben, could you maybe blow that filthy smoke out a window or someplace?" inquired Molly from her position up in the driveseat. "I never thought before I was allergic to smoldering seaweed, yet it seems—"

"All you need do, child," he told her in his rumbling catman voice, "is activate the aircirc system once again and—"

"The last time I did that Snif had a sneezing fit."

"Since the dear little fellow is wearing a fur suit, I don't imagine a gentle draft of chill air is likely to—"

"Nix, I don't want horrendous gusts of frigid air whistling across my toke," protested the disguised robot hound. "Bad enough I was forced into donning a sissy poodle costume so as to—"

"The real Alonzo Yapp, noted media mogul, never travels anywhere without at least one surly poodle in tow," reminded Jolson, shifting into his own voice. "Hence, I need one too."

Molly, who was wearing a platinum wig and a trim sinleather chauffeur uniform, said, "I know he also likes to have nubile blonde ladies drive his landcars and skycars, but I think we could bring off this latest impersonation of yours—especially since we're out here in the sticks—without so much darn attention to detail. I look awful as a blonde."

"Not any worse than I look as a poodle."

"Skipping the details can screw everything up." Jolson glanced out the one-way seethru window on his right.

The landlimo was whizzing along a wide highway that passed through vast plains. The grain was stunted and withered, and dark carrion birds were circling low over the blighted fields.

"You paid attention to details up in The Islands, dimwit, and they saw through your act anyway. So why—"

"We'll be at the outskirts of Triggersville in about ten minutes, Sniffer. Drop the conversation and start gnawing on that nice prop milkbone I got for you."

"Bones are high on the list of things I loathe. Though not as high as the name Ben Jols—"

"Looks like some sort of trouble in those fields over there." Molly slowed their landlimo.

Up ahead on the left a neowood barn was rapidly burning, sending great sooty spirals of smoke up into the waning afternoon. Some of the surrounding fields of dying grain were on fire as well. A dozen men in farm garb were strung out at the edge of the roadway, firing kilguns and lazguns at a scatter of men in bizsuits who were sheltered down behind an overturned landvan.

"Merely a disagreement between some insolvent farmers and their creditors," said Jolson in his Alonzo Yapp voice. "Keep right on moving, child, don't slow down."

"But people are likely to get—"

"Yapp is one of the most successful communications tycoons in the Barnum System," Jolson reminded, taking another puff on his cigar. "He takes no interest in a local frumus."

"You really are in a nasty mood today." She picked up speed and they drove right on by the roadside conflict.

"I'll wager," observed Sniffer, "that if there was even one blonde skwiff out there, he'd have been out of the car already."

Smoking his vile cigar, Jolson watched the ruined farmland they were rolling through.

A few moments later Molly said, "We're going to have to stop this time, Ben. There are a hundred people at least up there blocking the darn road completely."

Molly braked their landlimo to a stop. "Those aren't weapons they're carrying," she observed.

"Musical instruments, kiddo." Sniffer had his paws on the headrest of her seat. "We're being welcomed to town by a brass band."

"That's sure going to make an unobtrusive entrance into Triggersville darn difficult."

"You forget," reminded Jolson, "that Alonzo Yapp never makes an unobtrusive entrance to any place."

The citizens on the roadway converged on the halted landlimo. About fifty of them were clad in bright blue-and-gold band suits and marching, more or less, in step while playing a brassy martial tune. The rest of the crowd consisted of catmen, lizardmen, birdmen, toadmen and humanoids in either farm attire or bizsuits. Several of the grinning welcomers held up handmade glosigns containing such sentiments as *Welcome Yapp!, Triggersville Loves Media Moguls!* and *Paper, Mister?*

"Just about everyone seems to have fallen for our cover story," said Molly. "That you're Yapp and you intend to add the *Triggersville Weekly Forum* to your list of faxpapers."

"My lone pixcall to the editor has precipitated quite a—"

"Malarkey, don't be a dork," said Sniffer. "I pixed the Chamber of Commerce, the Triggersville Boosters Club, the Holy Name Sodality, the Friends of the Library and assorted other rube groups. That's what PR is all about. Makes the impersonation much more convincing, and if you had a brain even as large as a gnat's gazookis, Jolson, you'd have—"

"Molly dear, run around and open my door," suggested Jolson in his Yapp voice. "I want to dismount and greet all these eager yokels."

"Oh, darn, yes, sorry. I keep forgetting I'm posing as your servant." She let herself out of the landlimo, smiled briefly at the crowd that had stopped a few feet from the gilded hood. Scooting to Jolson's door, she made a small deferential bow and opened it. "We've arrived, Mr. Yapp, sir."

"Why, so we have, child." He huffed, groaned, got his catman bulk free of the rear seat. As he came tottering clear he patted Molly on the buttocks. "You're looking exceptionally trim, dear girl."

"Is the fondling necessary?" she inquired in a whisper.

"An essential part of the act." He patted her again, then stood taking in the blare of the band.

A hefty owlman in top hat and three-piece tuxsuit signaled the bandmaster with a feathery hand. The music stuttered, rattled to an uneven stop, faded away.

Inflating his broad chest, the owlman took several steps toward Jolson and Molly.

"I take it, sir, that I have the distinct pleasure of addressing the noted Alonzo Yapp."

"Yes, that you—oof!"

Sniffer had leaped out of the landlimo and up into Jolson's arms. "Don't forget your most important prop, deadhead," he muttered.

Jolson tightened a hand around the disguised dog's throat. "I am, indeed, Alonzo Yapp, and allow me to say, if I may, that it's a pleasure for me to visit your city, a city that I've often heard of."

"Don't shovel it on so—awk!"

After tightening his grip on Sniffer, Jolson asked the owlman, "Would you be the mayor of this impressive city?"

"Ah, yes, that's right. I am, yes." The owlman fluffed his facial feathers with both hands. "Forgive me for neglecting to introduce myself earlier. I am, sir, Raymond Wompertz, lord mayor of Triggersville."

"Your fame," said Jolson, "has spread far beyond the boundries of Triggersville, and your reputation for wise and compassionate decisions has reached me and those in the upper echelons of my organization."

"Oh, really? Why, that's marvelous," said Lord Mayor Wompertz with a chuckle. "I mean to say, I only took office a week and a half ago—to fill the unexpired term of poor Lord Mayor Chastain, who took an unfortunate header into his cider press. Still, though, I have made several wise and compassionate decisions since I moved into the octagonal office and assumed the mantle—"

"We've enjoyed a pleasant, though somewhat fatiguing, road journey, Mr. Mayor," cut in Jolson. "If you might escort us to our hotel, we'd like to—"

"Ah, yes, to be sure. Just as soon as we present you with the key to the city." He beckoned a large frogman in white bib overalls who'd been standing nearby with a large, tarnished silver key clutched to his chest. "Allow me to introduce High Sheriff Reisberson, who'll make a short official speech of—"

"I am related to *that* Reisberson," said the high sheriff, coming forward and holding out the big key. "We might as well get that all out in the open before we go on with all this folderol."

"Which Reisberson?"

"You know dang well which one," said the frogman. "The one they named Reisbersonitis after. Have you any notion of what it's like to have the same name as a disgusting, unpleasant disease? I doubt it, even though you have a pretty silly name yourself. I can still recall the fateful day that I, a sweet-tempered little tot, went toddling off to kindergarten, little realizing that my schoolmates were lying in wait to taunt me, to ridic—"

"Earl, you can go into the details of your childhood at the banquet tonight, perhaps," said Lord Mayor Wompertz, taking hold of the frogman's arm. "Right now, just hand over the dang key."

Reisberson lowered his head, contemplated his heavy yellow boots. "Yep, I'm right sorry, Mr. Yapp," he apologized. "Letting my own personal grief get in the way of—"

"Not at all, Sheriff, not at all. An important part of the Yapp Multi-Communications philosophy is to pay attention to the problems of each and every—"

"Stop! Halt!"

"Whatever is that?" The owlman scowled back at the crowd.

Someone was pushing his way through the idling band.

"Make way! This is urgent!"

Two birdman trombone players were shoved out of the way and a hefty catman stepped into view. Well dressed, he was an exact replica of Jolson as he looked at the moment, an exact replica of Alonzo Yapp.

"That man," said the newcomer, pointing an accusing furry finger at Jolson, "is a complete and total impostor! Sheriff, do your duty and arrest him at once!"

CHAPTER 17

Dropping Sniffer and smiling a shade sadly, Jolson thrust his hand into his jacket and went hurrying over to the finger-pointing intruder. "Nice try, Trumbower," he said in a low voice as he slipped his free arm around the shoulders of the other man. "But I don't have time to be sidetracked."

"I'm the real Alonzo Yapp! This man is—"

Zzzzzuuuummmmmmm!

Without letting the drawn stungun out of his jacket, Jolson had fired it at the other Alonzo Yapp.

The big catman stiffened, gnashed his teeth, collapsed against Jolson.

Jolson called out, "Give me a hand with Cousin Phil, will you, please, Nurse Briggs."

"Oh, yes, of course." Molly ran over to help him support the unconscious man. "He's had another of his spells, has he?"

"I fear so." With Molly on one side and himself on the other he hauled the stunned catman, feet dragging, over to the landlimo. He got him tossed in across the backseat.

"If this is the real Yapp," Molly said close to his ear, "we're in a heck of a lot of—"

"The real Yapp is on Jupiter buying a girls' softball team. We checked, remember?"

"Yes, but—"

"Cease fretting." Jolson slammed the door on the unconscious man, faced the puzzled, murmuring crowd and raised both hands high. "Pray forgive me for this unseemly intrusion." Grinning a bit forlornly, he walked over to pat the frogman sheriff on the back. "You're not the only one with a family curse, my boy."

"That fellow's a relative?" asked the mayor.

"Yes, my dear cousin, Philip K. Yapp. You may have noticed a moderate resemblance between the two of us," said Jolson. "He has lucid moments, yes, but lately his delusion that he's me has become more frequent. His fainting spells are also, regrettably, on the increase."

"Thought I heard a funny buzzing just afore he keeled over," said the high sheriff. "Almost like a stun—"

"That's poor Phil's plaz heart acting up," explained Jolson.

"Mr. Yapp, you really must stop letting your emotions override logic," put in Molly, shaking her head sympathetically. "You're going to have to have the fellow put away."

"Granted he causes me a considerable amount of embarrassment, as he's just done in front of the good people of Triggersville," he said with a deep sigh, "but after all, damn me, Phil is my kith and kin and when not ridden by his demons a very efficient galactic public accountant and a fine amateur saxophone player."

"I got a cousin who thinks, sometimes, he's a doorknob," volunteered one of the tenor sax players from the loitering band.

"Then you know what it's like." Jolson reached out, took the key to the city out of the hand of the still somewhat perplexed high sheriff. "Thank you for the kind reception, one and all. Now, if you can clear us a pathway, we'll drive on to our suite at the Sheldorf Hotel. Once there the efficient Nurse Briggs can attend to my deluded cousin."

Clearing his throat and clacking his bill, the mayor produced a voxcard. "My wife's cousin runs a discreet rest home a few miles out of town, should you—"

"DON'T WORRY ABOUT YOUR GOOFY LOVED ONES!" boomed the talking business card. "LOCK THEM AWAY AT MERLE'S SANITARIUM! ABSOLUTELY ESCAPEPROOF AND—"

Jolson popped the card in his pocket, silencing it. "Perhaps, should all else fail, we'll call on Merle, Lord Mayor Wompertz," he said. "And now, a temporary farewell until we meet again." With considerable dignity he waddled over to the gleaming landlimo and stood waiting.

Molly blinked, snapped her fingers, ran over. "Darn, I keep forgetting." She snatched the door open.

After elbowing the sprawled catman over to the far side of the compartment, Jolson grunted in and sat.

Sniffer hopped in after him, perching on his lap. "Where am I supposed to light now that this bozo has usurped my—"

"Try the floor." Jolson picked him up by his fuzzy scruff, deposited him at his feet. He shut the door and sat back.

Sniffer made a few disgruntled growling noises, then

nudged the snoring catman's leg with his nose. "You think this goon is really Wally Trumbower, the renegade Chameleon Corps agent who flummoxed you so recently up in The Islands?"

"We'll find out for certain once we get him to our suite." He dropped the key to the city down next to the robot dog.

Molly climbed in, started the engine. "That was very scary for a while."

"It was," he agreed. "Now get us the hell away from here."

Sniffer rolled over on his back, thrashing around on the thick dust-colored carpet of their living room. "Moll, assist me in getting out of this sissy poodle suit," he requested, paws working at the zipper on the belly of the furry disguise.

"Wait your turn," she said, helping Jolson prop the still-slumbering Wally Trumbower in an inflated rubberoid armchair. "He's still in his Alonzo Yapp mode, Ben. Are you absolutely sure we haven't gone and knocked out the authentic Alonzo—"

"Chameleon Corps agents, ex-Chameleons and renegade CC agents hold on to their assumed identities even when out cold," said Jolson, crouching next to the purple armchair. "Otherwise they'd give themselves away every time they got conked, drugged or stunned. Ask your pop."

"All this CC lore is terribly fascinating." The dog's paws were worrying at the zipper tab. "But I'm anxious to shed this particular identity. So, Molly, would you—"

"You're only going to have to put it all back on when we go outside," she told him while watching Jolson take a small drugkit from an inner pocket.

"Can't a bloke relax and slip out of his working togs in the privacy of his own room?" Sniffer writhed on the floor a few times. "Some penthouse suite this turned out to be, by the way. On the third floor. Geeze Louise, do these reubens actually think that—"

"Be still," she advised the dog.

Taking a small needlegun from the kit, Jolson inserted two different drug shots into it. "One to awaken Wally, the other to persuade him to tell all." He rolled up the sleeve of a jacket that was fairly similar to his, found a likely spot on the fat furry arm and touched the barrel of the gun to it.

Kzing! Kzang!

The catman in the chair sneezed twice, sat up, blinked his amber eyes. "Looks like this round goes to you, Jolson."

"Evens things up, Wally. You were Jody Pearl, weren't you?"

A grin touched his furry face. "Damn convincing, huh? I do great scatterbrained heiresses," Trumbower admitted. "I don't know why you never try female—"

"What you have coursing through your veins is Truthjuice number 104/P," explained Jolson, holding up the needlegun in his right paw. "There's no antidote, no way to provide advance immunity. You have to tell me the truth."

Trumbower's eyes narrowed as he checked that notion out. "Right you are, Jolson," he said. "Ask away, but keep in mind that I've treated you in a gentlemanly fashion. By stunning you instead of killing you, by alerting your pretty little boss here as to where she could find you. Those are—"

"Who're you working for?"

"A group."

"Group of what?"

"Concerned politicians and businessmen," answered the mind-controlled agent. "All of them had dealings with the recently ousted Prime Minister Saticoy and they really don't wish his political archives to be made public. That's the only portion of Starpirate's buried treasure they're interested in."

"Did you follow Flame Flenniken here to Farmstead Territory?"

"Yoo-hoo," whispered Sniffer, nuzzling against Molly's left leg. "Just give a tug at the lower extremities of this trick suit. I'm nearly out of the uppermost part."

"Okay, okay, but don't keep interrupting."

Trumbower said, "I followed the lady, yes. She's got the brainchip and Rudy Balooka."

"Where is she right now?"

"Out at the fairgrounds."

"Is that where the loot is hidden?"

"She seems to think so. She and her gang have been digging up the place since yesterday."

"Doesn't High Sheriff Reisberson object?"

"The fairgrounds has been abandoned for years; nobody goes near it anymore."

"Why aren't you there?"

"Apparently the info they got from Jackland Boggs's brain wasn't too specific. They don't seem to know the exact hiding place. So I gambled I had time to come to town, throw a spanner in your plans and then scoot back."

"How'd you know I was coming here as Alonzo Yapp?"

"I've got informants in town, Jolson. Soon as one of

them told me Alonzo Yapp was coming to purchase the local newssheet, I got a hunch. I tend to do pretty ladies, whereas you've always favored millionaires, billionaires, playboys and such. Besides, a smart tycoon like Yapp wouldn't even buy a copy of the local rag from a newsbot, and he sure as hell wouldn't buy out the whole enterprise."

"Did I not mention that?" mentioned Sniffer smugly, shedding the last of the poodle disguise and capering around on the rug. "It was highly improbable for Alonzo Yapp to—"

"They have a couple of swell closets in this room," warned Molly.

"Thus is the voice of reason ever stilled." He padded to the Lucite sofa, hopped atop it.

Jolson walked once around the drugged Trumbower. "Okay, what about Professor Tincan?"

"He's looking for the brainchip too. One of several competitors we have."

"Is he in Triggersville?"

"Got a convoy of gambling vans set up across the tracks. But I'm near certain Tincan doesn't know that Flame Flenniken is here and digging," answered the catman. "His sources of information aren't anywhere near as good as mine."

"But he's here."

"Somebody, possibly one of Starpirate's old crew, probably slipped him a hint that part of the missing loot was hidden hereabouts. That's why he's in the vicinity."

"He had a gent called the Whispering Gorilla on the trail of the brainchip."

"The Whispering Gorilla's here too. I'd guess they've

decided to go straight for the loot itself, but that's only a guess."

Jolson eyed his erstwhile Chameleon Corps colleague. "You didn't kill me up in The Islands," he said slowly, "yet back on Barnum you rigged an andy to do me in. And you knocked off Maybelle Vexford."

"Nope. I don't like working with robots or androids, Jolson. You can never trust them not to futz up at an important—"

"At least mechanisms don't get snookered into obvious traps that—"

"Don't interupt, Sniffer."

"A fake Dr. Chowderman called on the Vexford woman," said Jolson. "That had to be you, Wally."

"It was, sure. But the old dear was attacked before I even arrived."

"There's no record of any other visitors."

"Be that as it may, Jolson old buddy, I did not murder Maybelle. Now, you know damn well I'm obliged to tell you nothing but the truth."

Letting out his breath, Jolson stepped back. "We're going to take our leave," he told Trumbower. "This palatial suite is registered to Alonzo Yapp. You are a dead ringer for the old gentleman, and you'll be staying here for the next day or so. Confined to your bed, suffering from a bout of Reisbersonitis and not to be disturbed in any way. A much-respected physician will so inform the hotel."

"That's hardly sporting, Jolson."

"Hardly," he agreed.

CHAPTER 18

Up ahead in the deepening dusk, across a dark weedy field, rose a tall, thin white pyramid. Beside it squatted a large white sphere.

"Our destination," announced Jolson, turning their rented landcar off the rutted country highway and onto a wide and even more rutted road that cut across the overgrown field to the Triggersville Fairgrounds.

"Those two architectural excrescences were dubbed the Trylon and the Perisphere by the gimcrackers who constructed this pesthole back when," pointed out Sniffer from where he was sprawled in the backseat. "Here's a map of the whole dismal area." After some internal whirring and ratcheting, a faxpaper sheet was extruded from a slot in the robot dog's silvery side.

Reaching back, Molly took the map. "This'll be helpful to us, Ben."

"To me." He pulled off the ruined roadway, parking in a stand of blue willows. "You and Snif are going to remain here until I—"

"Crikey," groaned Sniffer, "don't you ever learn, beanpole? Each and every time you go blundering in solo, you end up flat on your toke or worse. What's really needed here is a little canine commando reconnoitering, to be provided by none other than—"

"We'll wait just fifteen minutes," Molly told him, brushing her red hair back. "Then we're coming after—"

"Half hour." He borrowed the map from her hand. "Trumbower says Flame Flenniken and associates were last seen exploring the area around the Hall of Industry. Yep, that's right here in the Court of Power, to the right of our Trylon and Perisphere."

"Pirates can be darn ruthless," she reminded him. "Be extra careful while you're sneaking up on—"

"I intend to." He eased the door open and stepped from the car. He was using his own identity again and was wearing a dark two-piece worksuit.

As he began walking through the high, crisp grass, three globats came skimming through the gathering twilight, flying low overhead.

Crouched low, he worked his way rapidly across the darkening field. Most of the high front wall that had surrounded the fairgrounds had long since fallen away. Jolson weaved through tumbled white neostone pillars, broken chunks of sudomarble. Tiny unseen rodents went scurrying out of his way, clicking deeper into the rubble.

Stopping beside a huge fallen statue of a winged grout, Jolson scanned the twilight acres. Off to the right of the towering Trylon, about a half mile or so away, he saw a scattering of small globes of light seemingly floating in the velvety darkness.

"Treasure seekers," he said to himself.

Crossing over what was left of the structure the map

labeled the Bridge of Wings, he then walked carefully along the Street of Wings. The once-white facade of Perylon Hall was streaked with blackish, faintly glowing fungus, and great jagged gaps showed in the walls.

Sprinting across the weed-spotted street, Jolson took a position against a low blank-walled building that had once housed an exhibition on the wonders of electronics. Ducked behind an overgrown hedge, he watched the bobbing lights a hundred yards away.

There were four lights—three lanternglobes and one lightstik—and four dark figures gathered around a hole in the middle of the street.

"Blimey," said a stunted frogman, gesturing excitedly and causing his lantern to dance, "we've finally struck something, lads. It's the ruddy treasure at last!"

"Stand aside." A broad-shouldered bearman lowered himself into the waist-deep hole. "It's a good-sized metal container, that's certain."

"Brush some of that dirt off the top of it," urged a crouching gatorman. "I do believe there's something inscribed on that container."

"Aye, there is." The bearman bent, made swift sweeping motions with one big paw.

Unnoticed, keeping close to the ruined walls and wild shrubs, Jolson worked closer to the preoccupied treasure hunters.

"I've heard tell of curses being inscribed on treasure chests."

"Give me a bit more light," requested the bearman; "my lightstik's going dim."

The frogman dangled his lantern into the hole. "I can make out the first word—'Greetings.' "

"That doesn't sound like the way you'd start off a curse," said the fourth pirate, a lean dogman. "Me, I believe I'd phrase it something like 'Woe betide any who dare—' "

" 'Greetings, citizens of the future,' " read the bearman in an increasingly growly voice. " 'You have unearthed the Triggersville Fair's Time Capsule, buried one thousand years ago and bearing the message of present-day Esmeralda to you people of a far-distant day.' "

"Why the bloody hell would Starpirate inscribe that on a container of hidden treasure?" inquired the perplexed frogman.

"He didn't, you roaring ninny." The angry bearman came growling up out of the hole, brushing dirt off himself. "What we've busted our tokes digging up for the last two and a half hours is the blasted time capsule the halfwits who staged this fair forty-some years ago stuck here."

"We oughtn't to have done that," said the dogman, shaking his head. "I was just a wee lad when my mum brought me to the fair, but I remember now that this here capsule was supposed to stay buried for a thousand years. We better cover it up again, so as not to spoil—"

"Can't you dolts even read our detecting gear rightly?" the bearman asked, glaring at the gatorman in particular. "We're looking for pirate loot, not blooming artifacts."

"Metal's metal," said the gatorman defensively. "And, as I told Flame back in the Home Show Pavilion, this equipment she saw fit to purchase for us isn't all that selective. Any buried metal—like those sewer pipes we dug up this morning, mates—is going to set it off."

"Never mind. We'll take a break for grub and grog before we try—"

"Oughtn't we," said the anxious dogman, "to bury this capsule again? A thousand or so years from now, they're probably going to come marching out here, school bands playing, dignitaries all gussied up, and they'll find just a gaping hole with maybe nothing down in—"

"Will we be around then?" growled the bearman. "Will we give a blinking snerg's arse what a bunch of—"

Zzzzzummmmmm!

Zzzzzzummmmmmm!

Zzzzzzzummmmmmm!

Zzzzzzzummmmmmm!

During the heated discussion Jolson had been able to get close enough to use his stungun.

The bearman toppled back into the hole, landing on the time capsule with a resounding bong.

The frogman teetered on the pit edge, then he, too, fell in.

The dogman took two steps backwards, sat, tumbled down.

The gatorman pivoted three times, arms flapping, before he dropped to the paving.

By the light of a dropped lantern Jolson consulted his map.

"*. . . she shivered and moaned, and I sensed the plea in her peepers. I danced my fingers over her yonkers before dislodging the frilly negligee—*"

"More bilge. Fast-forward it, Rudy."

"I got to tell you, Miss Flame, that a good deal of what's stored in Boggs's brain seems to be of a similar nature."

"There's got to be more about where exactly he stashed the plunder at this particular location."

"Meaning no offense, I'm sure, Miss Flame, but to really zero in on the contents of Starpirate's brain we need much more sophisticated and efficient equipment. This brainbox you bought ain't even as good as the one I was using in The Islands."

"Baloney. The clerk at Madman Milman's assured me this is as good as any of the higher-priced—"

"A bloke who's slogan is 'He's insane and so are his prices!' ain't exactly somebody I'd trust too—"

"Try again."

"Her emerald skin glowed invitingly in the moonlight and I felt the surging lift of her pretty-pretties as she pressed close against me. A lustful look crossed her kisser and—"

"More bushwah. Stop it again, Rudy."

Pressed against a still-standing wall of the Home Show Pavilion, Jolson edged closer to the jagged rectangle of light that had been a doorway, forty-some years ago.

Inside the dimly lit room Flame Flenniken and the captive birdman, Balooka, were apparently tuning in on the thoughts stored in the Jackland Boggs brainchip. The gleaning of the contents of Starpirate's mind was not, from the sound of it, going smoothly.

"Ah, wait a moment, Miss Flame. I've just now spotted a little dingus I hadn't noticed before. If I flip this, then mayhap we can instruct this cut-rate brainbox to do a bit more sorting for us and spew out only treasure-trove thoughts."

"Then flip the damn thing."

"Don't bother," advised Jolson, stepping into the room out of the night. He held his stungun ready.

Flame Flenniken, dressed in black as she had been when he'd briefly glimpsed her before, was sitting on a weather-beaten flowered sofa that still had a sign dangling above it that announced *The Sofa of the Future!* Her guns were holstered.

Balooka, the reedy little birdman, was crouched over a plaz coffee table upon which rested a small brainbox. "Say, now, the missus and I was just sitting around recalling better times, chum," he said. "We'd appreciate it if you'd scram and—"

"Very slowly and very carefully," instructed Jolson, "you pick up the brainbox and heft it over here to me."

"Ar, you don't want this one. No, we purchased this one off Madman Milman and it's a cheap knockoff of—"

"You're right, Balooka. What I actually want is the brainchip you swiped from Dr. Chowderman's establishment. C'mon, tote the box over to me."

Flame said, "Don't make a move, Rudy."

"Well, now, Miss Flame, I'm not exactly a willing coconspirator in this caper. Since this chap's carrying a weapon and seems—"

"Are you working for Professor Tincan?" the scarlet-haired pirate asked Jolson.

"Not at all."

"Well, hell, whoever's paying you, I'll offer more. Why be a simp and pass up the chance to make—"

Zzzzzuuuuuummmmm!

A stungun had suddenly been fired.

It was not Jolson's.

The beam of it slammed him square in the back. He lost all interest in debating with lady pirates and instead slumped to the muddy carpet and passed out.

CHAPTER 19

The sunflower was dirty and flat. After scrutinizing it for nearly a full minute, Jolson realized it was part of the pattern of the rug he was sprawled out on. Sucking in air, along with a little lint and dust, he tried to push himself up off the floor. His arms made odd creaky noises, but he managed to rise up to a kneeling position.

He was still in the Home Show Pavilion. A lone globe-lantern sat on the coffee table. Flame Flenniken, Rudy Balooka and the brainbox containing the Starpirate brain-chip were gone.

His stungun was on the stained rug. Bending to pick it up caused pain to go zigzagging through his skull and down his spine. Nonetheless, he managed to retrieve the weapon and return it to his shoulder holster.

When he finally got himself boosted to a standing position, the pains in his head and back grew worse. It took several minutes for the discomfort to subside. Eventually, very cautiously, he was able to go walking out into the night.

Deep darkness had spread throughout the fairgrounds,

and not a single light glowed anywhere. The sky was overcast.

The hole was still in the road where the pirates had been digging, and the time capsule was down there. But the four men Jolson had stunned had disappeared.

Out beyond the ruined gateways he saw his landcar where he'd parked it among the trees. When he noticed that the door on the passenger side was hanging open, he started running for the car.

Molly wasn't there.

Neither was Sniffer.

As he made a slow, careful circuit of the deserted vehicle, he heard a sound off in the darkness.

"Oy." Someone was moaning low. "Oy."

He drew his stungun, approached the moaning.

"Oy, woe."

Under a tree, flat on his back with his legs stiff in the air, lay Sniffer. His plaz eyes were glowing faintly orange and staring up into the dangling branches of the blue willow.

"Snif?" Jolson crouched beside the fallen robot hound. "Where's Molly?"

"Oy, woe, oy."

Putting his gun away, Jolson fished a compact electroscrewdriver from a pocket. He removed a small panel on the robot dog's belly and, using the light built into the screwdriver's tip, took a look at Sniffer's control center. "Somebody used a disabler gun on you," he said, nodding. "Then tossed you into the bushes."

"Oy," moaned the stricken dog.

Concentrating, Jolson poked and probed. He reattached wires, mended a thin twist of cable, reset dials and switches that the disabler had glitched. "That ought to do it for now." He put the stomach plate back in place.

"If you're through sticking your clammy mitts into my secret places, Jolson," said Sniffer, "I'd like to roll over onto my feet and get cracking."

"You're welcome."

"Okay, sweetheart, thanks for patching me up."

"Skip the heartfelt gratitude and tell me where Molly is."

Sniffer stood, wagged his tail, shook himself a few times. "Well, I'm a mite chagrined about this."

"Just explain."

"They got the drop on us. Used a stungun on Molly, a disabler on me."

Jolson and the dog returned to the car. "Who were they?"

"The nurf who decked me and then gave me the old heave-ho into the foliage must've been your old pal the Whispering Gorilla," answered Sniffer. "The three other shrabs I haven't been able to ID as yet. Weren't any goons we've encountered before."

"They either trailed us here or got wind that Flame Flenniken was treasure-hunting in these parts."

"Was she?"

"She was, and she had Starpirate's brain."

Sniffer hopped into the landcar through the open doorway. "I take it the noted lady buccaneer of the spaceways isn't around anymore."

"Somebody stungunned me while I was talking to her and Balooka." He slid into the driveseat. "When I awoke, she was gone."

"You're even sappier than I am. Letting them get the drop on—"

"We both did less than admirably," acknowledged Jolson, starting the engine. "Since the Whispering Gorilla is employed by Professor Tincan, it seems likely they've taken Molly to his Kasino Karavan. Which is where we're going."

"Good idea, but, geeze, try not to act like a nitwit when—"

"We'll both strive for that."

Big and green now, Jolson went stomping up the metallic steps of the main casino van. He kicked the door open wide with a heavy, booted foot, sending the tuxsuited gatorman who'd been stationed behind the slot in the door dancing backwards across the carpeted floor of the narrow mobile gambling den.

The gatorman was executing desperate wigwags with his arms, striving to maintain his balance. Efforts failing, he fell over onto a sparsely attended craps table. The dice, just thrown by an obese catman in sea-blue bib overalls, jumped clear of the green-topped table, clicked together twice in midair and went plummeting to the floor.

"Made my point," said the catman, pointing at them where they'd hit.

"Ar, you lop-eared tubeswabbers," roared Jolson in a gruff, gargly voice, "keep your flippers in view or, so help me Hannah, I'll slice off your gullyrakers." He had one big green hand under his long bronze beard and the other resting on the butt of the kilgun holstered on his right hip.

Two burly dogman bouncers in tight-fitting tuxsuits had been making their way through the smattering of patrons. Halting a few yards away, they grinned and wagged the empty paws that they'd just yanked out from under their jackets.

"You, you walleyed pillicock," Jolson bellowed at the burlier of the two bouncers.

"Yeah, what?"

"Tell that rust-ridden beantosser, Professor Tincan, that I want to see him."

The dogman shrugged, squinted. "And who the blue blazes might you be, uncle?"

Giving out an annoyed roar, Jolson announced, "I am Jackland Boggs, you half-witted crannyhaunter."

"Yipe!" remarked one of the dented robot blackjack dealers, cards flying out of his grasp as he dropped suddenly out of sight behind his table. "It's Starpirate!"

"Starpirate!"

"Holy moley, this guy's Starpirate!"

"Who the dickens is Starpirate?" asked the obese catman farmer, addressing a gambler who'd just thrown himself flat out on the far side of the craps table.

"Only just the scourge of the spaceways, buddy."

The burlier dogman bouncer started to shiver some. "Um . . . truly sorry I didn't recognize you, Jackland . . . um, Mr. Boggs . . . um, Mr. Starpirate."

"Cease your nattering and take me to Tincan pronto."

The dogman's arm quivered as he raised it to point at a silvery door across the small casino. "He's . . . um . . . he's in his office over there, sir."

Before Jolson, striding with wide floor-stomping steps, reached the silver door, it opened narrowly.

The Whispering Gorilla, clad in a crimson tuxsuit,

edged out into the portable casino. "Stop right there, jocko," he advised in his low raspy voice.

"Out of my way, you peabrained mowdiwart."

"Listen, my friend," confided the gorillaman, reaching out to take hold of Jolson's arm, "we have reason to believe you can't be the genuine art—"

Zzzzzzummmmmmmm!

Without taking his left hand from beneath his massive coppery beard, Jolson had fired the stungun concealed thereunder.

Dodging the falling gorilla, he stepped over him, kicked open the door to Professor Tincan's private office and entered.

Professor Tincan had the top of his chrome-plated humanoid head open wide. He was in the process of taking his flesh right hand out of his head and dropping it toward the kilgun sitting atop his desk next to the stolen brainbox. "You've got some nerve, Boggs—or whoever you are," he said in his high-pitched tinny voice. "Storming in on a guy while he's performing intimate acts with his noggin and—"

"Don't touch the gun, you bowlegged tugmutton." Jolson drew his stungun from under his crinkly whiskers.

The greenish plaz-walled office was small and the metal-headed cyborg was the only one conscious when Jolson arrived.

Molly was slumped in a tin armchair just under the room's small, high glaz window. Flame and Balooka were tangled together on a fat water sofa.

"A few of my customers have passed out," explained Professor Tincan, gesturing at the stunned trio. "A physician is on the way, and if you'll step outside it will facilitate—"

"You swiped my brain," accused Jolson.

"This is hardly the expression of gratitude I expected. WG and I—WG is my nickname for the Whispering Gorilla. WG and I were tipped that this red-haired bimbo—the red-haired bimbo on the sofa, not the red-haired bimbo in the armchair—that Flame Flenniken had come into possession of your brain. Naturally we, aiming to do you a favor, set about—"

"I want the brainchip back."

"You're not paying attention, Boggs. Well, if you are Boggs, that figures, since you're not supposed to have a functioning brain at all. What I'm trying to convey is simply that, at great risk, we rescued your brainchip from mean-minded space looters. We then transported the precious chip here for safe—"

"You were about to stick the chip in your own conk," said Jolson, snarling. "That isn't my notion of safekeeping."

Reaching up, Professor Tincan shut his skull. "Actually, SP—may I call you that, SP, short for Starpirate? Actually, SP, I was suffering from a mild headache, and I've found that a bit of fresh air on the old brain works wonders with—"

"I'll be taking the chip now," Jolson told him, "and the young lady."

"Which young lady?"

"The one in the armchair."

"Looks a bit on the skinny side to me, SP. If I were picking, I'd probably go for Flame Flenniken. She's meatier and, from all I hear, a bit lusty in her—"

"Slide the brainbox across to me."

The plaz eyes in the metallic head blinked several times. "Certainly, to be sure. Take it, SP, and welcome to it. No hard feelings, and hopefully someday we can get together to work a scam or—"

"You're giving up the box too willingly," said Jolson, eying him. "Leading me to believe the chip isn't in it any longer."

"If it isn't, SP, then I have no idea where—"

"I'd prefer you to hand the thing over." Jolson shifted the stungun to his left hand, yanked the kilgun from its holster. "At my age, I no longer much enjoy frisking a corpse. But I will unless you turn the brainchip over right now."

"I might as well level with you, SP," said Professor Tincan. "I've already inserted the brainchip in my skull to augment my own humble brain. Not, let me assure you, so I'd know where all your pirate loot is hidden. But only so that I might have the benefit of the vast criminous knowledge you've amassed during—"

"The brainchip."

The cyborg picked up a pair of electrotweezers. He popped his metal skull open again, inserted the tweezers and extracted the brainchip. Shutting his skull, he returned the chip to the brainbox. "No hard feelings, SP?"

Jolson tucked the brainbox up under his left arm. He backed to the tin armchair and started to slip his right arm around the unconscious Molly.

That was when Professor Tincan decided to make another try for his kilgun.

Zzzzzuuummmmm!

The pane of the room's only window came falling down,

landed on the desk, bounced, flipped over onto the floor to land with a faint whapping sound. By that time Professor Tincan had fallen forward, his head bonging on the desktop.

Sniffer's glittering head appeared up at the opening. "I'm not even going to mention that I've just saved your bacon," he said. "Had I not, however, been hovering up here, ever on the alert, that jughead would've fried your—"

"And I intend to be eternally grateful, Snif," Jolson assured him as he lifted Molly up. "Now go wait in the car."

CHAPTER 20

Molly sat up on the scarlet heart-shaped bed. Glancing up, she noticed the pink-tinted heart-shaped mirror in the crimson ceiling and brushed at her tousled auburn hair. "Ben," she said quietly, "you must've rescued me. Thanks."

He was sitting in a plump crimson armchair, one with an overstuffed heart-shaped back, that he'd pulled over near her bedside. "Professor Tincan and his cronies had grabbed you." He tucked his drugkit away in his coat pocket. He'd changed clothes and was himself again. "We also got hold of Starpirate's—"

"Where's Sniffer? Did they hurt—"

"I'm invulnerable, sis," called the robot hound from where he was stretched out on a pink sofa across the room. "But Slimjim wouldn't allow me to approach whilst he was shooting you full of quack drugs and—"

"Well, I'm darn glad we all survived." Taking hold of Jolson's hand, she squeezed it.

"We've got Starpirate's brain," Jolson repeated, nodding toward the brainbox reposing on the heart-shaped coffee table. "So, soon as you're completely recovered, we can head for our client to deliver—"

"Where exactly are we right now?"

"Still in Farmland Territory."

Molly glanced around the scarlet-hued room. "This place has a sort of low-life feel to it."

"What do you expect," queried Sniffer, "from a joint that calls itself the No Questions Asked Motel?"

"There are going to be all sorts of people on our tail eventually," said Jolson. "This sounded like a place that can be discreet about—"

"The Haymow Skytel looked a lot snazzier," observed the dog.

Jolson was frowning at the young woman. "You shouldn't be at all groggy," he said. "The shot I gave you not only revives, it wipes out the aftereffects of a stungun blast."

"I'm not groggy. Not at all. Why are you accusing me of being groggy?"

"Mostly because you haven't reacted at all to that fact that we're now in possession of the object we've been seeking. Starpirate's brain." He leaned closer, watching her. "All we do now is deliver it to Preston Zuck in Jazinto Territory, collect the rest of our fee and troop to the spaceport. A comfortable spaceliner whisks us home to Barnum, we shake hands and I return to the ceramics trade."

Instead of replying, Molly swung off the bed. She smoothed her wrinkled skirt, crossed to the open door of the bathroom. "Good gosh!" she exclaimed.

"What?" He started to get up.

"Even the toilet seat's shaped like a heart."

"There's romance everywhere at the No Questions Asked Motel." Sniffer rolled his plaz eyes.

Jolson stood. "Molly, before you go on to catalog the rest of the heart shapes in the room," he said evenly, "explain why you're being evasive."

"I'm not being evasive," she replied. "After all, I have suffered through a heck of a lot lately. Had to pretend to be a sex-crazed chauffeur, got stungunned by a gorilla with laryngitis, wake up in a bedroom that'd have to be spruced up a lot before it could even be classed a bordello crib. No wonder, is it, Ben, that I'm having trouble thinking straight?"

"Whenever I mention heading for home," persisted Jolson, "you take on an uneasy look. We were hired to locate Jackland Boggs's missing brainchip. We've done that."

Molly, folding her arms, leaned in the bathroom doorway. "Well, there are a couple aspects of this case we haven't discussed maybe as thoroughly as we should've, Ben."

"Such as?"

"Keep in mind that, although we're good friends—real pals, in fact—I happen to be, after all, a partner in the whole darn BIDS operation." She glanced again up at the ceiling mirror. "You, good friend and real pal that you are, are still just an employee of the agency. So actually my father and I aren't obliged to confide every little bit of—"

"What have you kept back from me, Molly?" He took three steps in her direction.

"This is getting exciting," observed Sniffer, sitting up. "I'm starting to think there's something afoot that even *I* wasn't aware of."

"Really, though," began Molly, unfolding and then refolding her arms, "it isn't all that momentous or anything."

"What is it?"

"Well, Preston Zuck happens to have Starpirate's power of attorney—got it passed to him after Maybelle Vexford expired. At the moment, therefore, until the brainchip's safely back in Boggs's own head, Preston Zuck pretty much can call the shots. What he's done is set up a very lucrative side deal, which will benefit Jackland Boggs a good deal."

Jolson took two steps back from her. "What sort of deal?"

"Seems the *Galactic Enquirer* is offering—incredible, isn't it, the sort of money these mass-circulation publications can toss around?—they're offering two million trudollars for the Saticoy documents and journals that Starpirate stole and hid away someplace with a portion of his loot."

"The Political Espionage Office isn't going to look favorably on—"

"That's why we're going to have to act darn fast on this."

"That political stuff could be at the fairgrounds or some other spot where he hid his plunder. You'd have to get access to a much more sophisticated brainbox than this one of Flame Flenniken's in order to sift through the contents of Starpirate's brain rapidly enough to—"

"Nix," put in Sniffer, "I've got all the sophisticated equipment you need built right in, state of the art." He tapped at his glittering forehead with a forepaw. "I just insert the chip in the slot in my left ear and—presto!—I'll be able to inform you exactly where the telltale Saticoy outpourings are concealed."

"Maybe the Saticoy stuff ought to be turned over to the government of this planet," said Jolson. "We don't even know—"

"The Esmeraldan government might simply suppress it," Molly pointed out. "Seems to me, really, that we're obliged to make sure the truth gets before the public so that—"

"How much?"

"What?"

"How much more is Preston Zuck offering you for doing this little job?"

"Well, two hundred thousand trudollars, but it's the quest for the truth that's the most important—"

"I'm going for a stroll." Jolson crossed, rapidly, the bedroom.

"It's raining out there," Sniffer pointed out.

"You're not thinking of quitting, are you, Ben?" asked Molly, watching him yank the door open.

"Be back in a while." He left the room, stepped out into the night.

Hunched, scowling, hands in pockets, Jolson walked slowly around the five-acre complex that housed the motel. The rain was warm, slow-falling.

He passed the No Questions Asked Café, which didn't seem to be doing much business, and then the No Questions Asked Roller Rink. The sound of a lone skater suddenly falling over came echoing hollowly out through the open doorway.

At the edge of the grounds, its back to the dark rainy

fields, sat the No Questions Asked Bookshop. There were wide strips of plaztape making big Xs across the store's two glaz front windows. On the glaz door was stuck a sign announcing *Business As Usual During Siege!*

Jolson entered. There didn't appear to be anyone on duty, and several odd odors assailed his nostrils. He sneezed twice while glancing around at the racks of faxbooks and faxmags.

"Arg yur gustim?"

He spun, still saw nobody. "Beg pardon?"

From behind the small dented checkout counter emerged a thin, frail ratman in a three-piece cazsuit and thick neowool pullover. He was wearing a gas mask. "Was I eggs us arg you gustim or wad?"

"I guess I'm a customer."

Sighing, the clerk removed the mask. "I noticed you were bothered by the odors in here."

"Can't quite figure what it is."

Holding up his left paw, the clerk started ticking off fingers. "Three nights ago they burned a stack of objectionable magazines," he explained. "That sooty smell is still lingering. Two different stink bombs were set off last evening, just about this time. When my cousin Earl opened up at midday today he found a dead grout in the storeroom." The ratman gave a sad laugh. "Have to admire their tactical abilities. I wouldn't have any idea how to get something as big as a dead grout snuck in here in broad daylight or—"

"Who's doing this?"

"Oh, a wide and colorful variety of special-interest groups," replied the ratman. "There's the rub with freedom of expression and a relatively open society. Just about anybody and his brother have the right to attack you." After carefully staring out into the night, he ventured from behind his counter. "Of course, my biggest problem is the girlie magazines. We stock over three hundred and forty, from dozens of planets."

"You mean you're having censorship troubles?"

"Oh, there's been some of that—mostly from the Peace and Freedom Party. They're fairly simpleminded, want to suppress all and sundry magazines that show any kind of nudity or sexual activity." He stopped by a magazine rack, gestured at the top row. "The big problem is what various people find offensive and what other people find stimulating. Take *Froggish Erotica* here. Frogmen, as you may or may not be aware, are excited by photos of sparely clad frogwomen in lacy pink lingerie. Toadmen—at least rural toadmen—believe it's a mortal sin to show any sort of woman in her underwear, especially if that underwear is pink. So they want *Froggish Erotica* burned. On the other hand, they demand that we stock *Toad Elbows.* The elbow, to a toad—to a rural toad anyway—is considered very sexy. Unfortunately, there are a lot of gatorman fundamentalists in the area, and they believe a naked elbow is an offense to God. Especially a green elbow, which is what both they and their God have. They're particularly concerned lest young gators chance in here and glimpse such material. I offered to put a sticker on each magazine —*For Mature Gators Only*—but that only riled them more and they tossed one of last evening's stink bombs."

"Who contributed the defunct grout?"

"That must've been, I'm near dead certain, the Buy Esmeralda Goods Advisory Board. They object to this skin mag here—*Humanoid Schoolgirls in Nothing but Frilly Sinsilk Underwear.*"

"Not a very catchy title."

"One of them discovered most of the schoolgirls were wearing underwear manufactured in the Earth System and they— Oopsy!"

Jolson turned to see what the clerk was staring at outside. Riding hell for leather across the rainswept night fields came a dozen black-robed, black-hooded riders. Some were mounted on horses, some on grouts. "More critics?"

The ratman had already ducked again behind his counter and was reaching for his gas mask. "It's the Holy Hill Hunt Club again," he warned, popping the mask in place. "Wadj oud."

CHAPTER 21

A grout is somewhat like a horse and somewhat like a cow and has six legs. The leader of the Holy Hill Hunt Club was mounted on a snorting white-and-brown one that he reined up on the walkway a hundred feet or so from the doorway of the No Questions Asked Bookshop. The other black-robed, black-hooded riders had pulled up further off.

The leader, whose hood was drooping some because of the night rain, held a megaphone in his right hand and a flamegun in his left.

"Ahum," he said into the black megaphone. "You in there—you know why we're here."

Jolson was squatting beside the ratman clerk and watching the raiders over the top of the counter. "Why are they here?"

"Id's uh relidjus comter . . ." He tugged his gas mask off. "This one's a religious controversy."

"We warned you about that heathen book," continued the leader of the Holy Hill Hunt Club. "All copies were to have been destroyed by this morning."

"We had to buy those books outright from the publisher," the clerk explained to Jolson. "Burning thirty-five damn copies means a loss of—"

"So we've come to burn them for you! Then we're going to burn your whole godless bookstore and, for good measure, your godless motel and, quite probably, your godless skating rink, souvenir shop and natural-food outlet."

"What book's he yelling about?"

The ratman made a cautious gesture toward the nearest rack. "It's a scholarly work entitled *The Evolutionary Impact of the Farmstead Man,*" he answered. "Has to do with some old bones that were dug up hereabouts a few years ago. Author claims the skeleton proves the denizens of this planet evolved and weren't, as many believe, created by God and Saint Reptillicus. Nobody would have paid much attention to this book except that a vidwall evangelist named Reverend Willy Dee Showcase has been attacking it in his sermons of late. Ever watch him?"

"Infrequently."

"We're going to count up to twenty-seven and then, should these infamous books not be heaped out here and burning merrily, we're coming in and we'll start a blaze that will serve as a lesson to all heathens in these parts."

Nodding to himself, Jolson took off his jacket and shirt. "Stay down," he advised the shivering clerk. "Put your mask back on and duck low."

"Might I inquire as to why you're stripping to the waist?"

"Don't want to split my coat or shirt. Duck."

The ratman slapped the gas mask on once more, stretched out on the floor and covered his head with both paws.

Concentrating, Jolson changed. His chest grew broader,

his arms thicker. His face turned porcine and his hair became golden and shoulder length. "We've got enough problems without these louts burning down the motel," he muttered as he stood up and flexed his mighty hairy arms.

Rumbling some in his meaty chest, Jolson went striding outside.

"I don't notice any offensive books in your—"

"Shut up, peckerhead!" said Jolson in a nasty gruff voice. His pinkish pig eyes were glaring, his bristly snout was twitching.

"Sir, you happen to be addressing the commander in chief of—"

"I'm addressing a big pile of groutcrap covered with a dirty sheet." He walked up close to the mounted man and pounded on his bare chest with a meaty fist. "Take a good look at me, peckerhead. Do you know me?"

The man adjusted his hood, shifting the position of the eyeholes. "Now you mention it, there is something familiar about your appearance, sir. However, I—"

"My name is Sissy Boy McYancy. Could be you've seen me on the vidwall."

"Why, yes, now that you mention it, that's it. You often come on the air immediately following Reverend Willy Dee Showcase's *Wambam Hour of Electronic Fingerpoppin' Prayer.* You're a professional wrestler."

"I'm the commander in chief of the meanest, rottenest six-man tag team in the universe, peckerhead," Jolson explained. "Now, before I get to my point—let me explain why they call me Sissy Boy."

"There's really no need for—"

"They call me Sissy Boy because of my relative gentleness. Once, when I ripped a gent's arm out of the socket,

I failed to whap him over the head with it thereafter," said Jolson, glowering up at the masked rider. "Another time a frail old birdlady cut in front of me in a shuttle line, and instead of cracking her spine I simply gave her a tap on the dome that gave her a mild concussion. Incidents like that affect your reputation, and that's how come I'm known as Sissy Boy."

"Yes, well, that's certainly—"

"My five partners are in temporary residence over yonder, peckerhead." He flexed his powerful right arm, pointed at the motel. "Fact is, we've splurged with some of our prize money and hired a hooker for the six of us. Disturbing them, which all this vigilante foolishness is on the brink of doing, is going to result in at least broken bones and severe head injuries. My associates include Ed 'Strangler' Cornwall, Babykiller Busino and Gutter Kaminsky, aka the Venusian Angel."

"Actually, Mr. Sissy Boy, we've taken care of just about all our business here," said the hooded rider. "Quite frankly, we do this sort of thing mostly for the exercise. Groutback riding is very good for—"

"Then exercise your butts in riding away," suggested Jolson. "Yeah, and if I find out you came back later to annoy my pals here, I might mention it to my partners. It's difficult to go through the remainder of your days with, for example, your innards dangling outside your body. A word to the wise."

"Surely, yes. We have many other good works to take care of, Mr. Sissy Boy. Wellsir, my two boys will certainly be elated when they hear I've met one of their favorites."

He jerked on the reins, got his grout turned and went galloping away.

The other raiders followed him off across the night fields.

After watching their swift departure for a moment, Jolson returned inside to retrieve his shirt and coat. He resumed his own identity and dressed.

The ratman, getting up from the store floor, stared at him. "That's quite a knack you have."

"It is."

"Must be terrific to be able to do that."

"It's a great comfort," said Jolson as he left.

The door of the motel suite opened as he reached for it.

"What was going on out there, Ben?" asked Molly, stepping back from the doorway.

"A rather lively literary discussion." He came in, crossed and sat on the sofa. "Where's Sniffer?"

"Oh, I put him in a closet." She seated herself beside him. "He can be very distracting at times."

Jolson's grin was bleak.

Molly said, "There are some things we ought to talk about. Earlier I was sort of bossy, and I'm sorry about that, Ben."

He studied her pretty face for a few silent seconds. "Most of the time I am, more or less, fond of you," he informed her. "But I don't much like it when you start acting tough and—"

"Well, I know. That's what, darn it, I'm trying to apologize to you about and—"

"What I enjoy even less are these moments when you try to charm me into doing something you think I don't want to do."

"Charm you?" She sat up, frowning. "Are you so self-centered as to imagine that I am, right now, you mean, trying to seduce you into something? Really, I should think I've made it pretty awfully clear that I'm not at all attracted by you, Ben. I admit that when I think you're seriously injured and then it turns out you aren't I do hug and kiss you. That's all just a brotherly-sisterly thing, and I assumed you understood. At the time that I was a foolish girl of eighteen I did have a crush on you, but that was eight years ago and—"

"Ten years ago." He stood. "Look, Molly, I'll stay on and help you unearth the Saticoy papers. So spare me the—"

"This is, you have my darn solemn word, the very last field assignment you and I are ever going to share." Folding her arms under her breasts, she turned away from him.

"Let us hope." He went to the door of his room and opened it.

CHAPTER 22

A vaguely familiar sound out in the chill grey morning caused Jolson to awaken and jump clear of his jelbed. Before the low heart-shaped bed had ceased quivering, he'd donned trousers and tunic and stepped into the next room.

Sniffer was stretched out on an oval throw rug, eyes shut. Scattered around him were sheets of faxpaper and a few maps and charts. There was an electropen near his right paw.

Molly's bed was empty and she wasn't about.

Crossing to the window, Jolson deblanked one pane and looked out into the day.

Zzzzzzmmmmmooooookkkkkkk!

There it was again. The sound of a Dorammer pistol. Seven hooded riders were galloping by the front of the No Questions Asked Roller Rink, shooting away doors and windows.

"I thought I warned those guys last night not to . . . Ah, a different band of vigilantes."

These raiders wore scarlet robes and hoods. One of them carried a glosign reading *Ban Coed Sports!*

He blanked the window, shrugged. "An entirely different debate."

"Having a little heart-to-heart talk with yourself, dimwit?"

Jolson sat on a heart-shaped bench and contemplated the reclining robot hound. "How soon before you sort through the clutter in Boggs's brain and find out where—"

"I've already done the necessary work." The dog tapped his collection of notes and maps. "The old boy sure dipped his wick in a lot of places. Even with my sophisticated scanning equipment, I had to wade through miles of sultry recollections. Were I so inclined I could now compile a fat dictionary of synonyms for the female breast. Having, however, a far better—"

"Where's the Saticoy material hidden?"

"We'll get to that soon. First allow me to conclude the snappy prologue so that—"

Zzzzzzzummmmmmmm!

Just outside the door of the suite someone had fired a stungun.

Jolson's hand was reaching for his shoulder holster when the door swung open.

Molly came backing in, clutching a large plyobag under her arm and waving her stungun. "That was sort of fun," she said, kicking the door shut.

"Did somebody try to—"

"Only a hooded twerp who came riding at me as I stepped from the No Questions Asked Café." After putting her gun away in her thigh holster, she placed the sack on the coffee table. "He implied I was a wicked woman and that he was going to groutwhip me. When the stungun beam hit him, he sailed clean out of his saddle. Darn gratifying."

"Sniffer's determined where—"

"You might at least pause, Ben, and tell me you're glad I wasn't trampled by a grout."

"I'm striving to be businesslike."

Sniffer was sitting on his haunches now. "Listen, folks, why not let me explain myself exactly what—"

"Before we have a conference," said Molly, sitting on the sofa, "I bought us breakfast, Ben. Sort of a gesture of reconciliation. Although if you're going to keep on being snide and grouchy—"

"Being businesslike isn't being snide and grouchy." He poked around in the bag. "Soy donuts and sinsausage?"

"The menu at the No Questions Asked Café is limited," she said. "The donuts are filled with homemade jelly. The waitress assured me that—"

"What say you two gourmands pipe down," suggested the dog. "Then we can get to the issue at hand without further de—"

"The donut on top is filled with papaya marmalade and the other one—"

"I don't want to hear about the other one." Jolson took the top donut.

"There's syncaf in there someplace, too. One plain and the other with—"

"Which do you want?"

"Doesn't matter."

Jolson lifted out a plazcup of imitation coffee. "Okay, Snif, fill us in."

"You're absolutely certain you don't want to babble on a bit longer? Exchange some recipes or—"

"Just because you don't require nutrients, Sniffer, is no reason to heckle us." Molly took a bite of her donut, wrinkled her nose, took another bite and then set the donut aside.

"Do I," inquired Sniffer as he scratched at a silvery ear with his hind paw, "have your undivided attention?"

"Get on with it." Jolson sipped at his syncaf.

"The currently brainless Mr. Boggs hid the assorted records of P.M. Saticoy's reprehensible political activities separately from any of his other space-pirate plunder," explained the robot dog. "He sensed that the stuff had blackmail possibilities and intended to allow it to ripen for a spell before putting it to use."

"Where," asked Jolson, "is it?"

"About five hundred miles south of here, in Pontapay Territory. At a spot that was remote and out of the way at the time, as well as being far from the beaten path and little frequented."

Molly asked, "But now?"

"Attend to me," invited Sniffer, "while I inform you about some difficulties that Starpirate didn't foresee."

CHAPTER 23

Roughly three minutes after Jolson's dressing room landed on the vast yellow plain, the young woman with the rainbow hair was whapping his door with both fists.

Sniffer scrutinized her through the one-way glaz door of the skyvan. "Skinny and unkempt," he remarked from his seat at the makeup table. "Obviously your type of wench, Benjy."

Jolson was now thin and black, possessed of spiked orange hair and large dangling earrings fashioned from glometal. His two-piece cazsuit was made of shimmering throbcloth and it blinked from glaring scarlet to glaring green. A half-dozen globracelets encircled each skinny black wrist. "She's with the press," he said with little enthusiasm, recognizing Timmy Tempest.

"Maybe," suggested Molly, who was wearing a dark wig and sitting in the pilot seat, "we ought to avoid the media. This latest ID of yours isn't the safest—"

"You can't avoid—"

"Hey in there, Billy!" shouted Timmy, stepping up the intensity of her two-fisted bamming on the door. "I've got to interview you for *Galactic Variety,* you nurf! Quit being aloof and let me in so we can get this over with!"

Nodding at Molly, Jolson settled into a licorice-hued Lucite chair. He picked up a silvery saxophone, arranged it across his sharp knees. "Let her in."

"How come it turns out I'm always the servant in these darn impersonations?" Rising, she went over to open the door.

"About time." Timmy barged into the large dressing room.

Outside behind her could be seen other skyvans and trailers, as well as security guards in blue unisuits and a mix of idling musicians and their hangers-on.

Molly asked, "What exactly do you—"

"Here's my card. Although, honestly, I should think—seeing as how you're Billy Poison's latest mistress—you'd know all the important show-biz reporters."

"Maybe I do." Molly didn't take the voxcard the rainbow-haired girl had produced from her purse.

"INTRODUCING MISS TIMMY TEMPEST," shouted the vocal business card, "REPORTER-AT-LARGE FOR *GALACTIC VARIETY!*"

"Clamjafry," muttered Jolson, scowling at the reporter.

"What's he talking ab—"

"INTRODUCING MISS TIMMY—"

"Enough already." She jammed the card into her lumpy purse.

Moving behind Jolson's chair, resting one hand on it, Molly said, "Billy wants you to know he doesn't have much time to—"

"*He* doesn't have time?" Timmy positioned herself in a tin rocker. "Listen, hon, I've got to do dippy interviews with Edward Everett Garbage and the Scavengers, Tunky Nesper, Bix Boparoony and the Bellhops, Constance Cleanhead and the Baldtones, Gatemouth Gonzer and a whole tedious stewpot of other slurpy musicians who're infesting this Fourth Annual Dopestix Jazz and Folk Musicon. All between now and suppertime. So don't go tell—"

"Tripe," grunted Jolson.

"He'd like you," urged Molly, "to get started."

Rolling her eyes and then winking at Sniffer, Timmy said, "This is really a fate worse than death. I mean, having to get enough for a hundred-word item out of this zombie is—"

"Slag."

"He's losing interest in—"

"Okay, okay. The first thing I'd like to know is where you've been for three years. It was reported that you died in a skycar crash on the planet Peregrine, Billy, although your fans have always maintained—half-wits that they are—you were merely disfigured and went into hiding."

"Offal."

"He'd prefer you address him as Mr. Poison."

"Sheesh. Okay, Mr. Poison, sir. What happened in that accident?"

"Rummage."

"He's still not ready to talk about that."

"Sounds to me like he's not ready to talk about anything." Timmy shifted impatiently in her seat. "How about his being here? His name wasn't on the official program, and the management of this simp circus only announced an hour ago that he—"

"Let me," volunteered Sniffer, "field that one."

Timmy glanced over at him. "Isn't that cute, a talking puppy. Gee, I wish I could afford one."

"I am not a puppy. I happen to be a highly sophisticated—"

"Billy Poison," said Molly, making shushing motions at the robot dog, "has two reasons for attending the Fourth Annual Dopestix Jazz and Folk Musicon here on Lyon's Plains. He wanted, firstly, to play for his public once again after his long and painful hiatus. And secondly, the Monastery of Saint Viper happens to sit in the middle of the plain where the festival'll be going on for the next two weeks. During his hiatus he became a convert to the teachings of Saint Viper and hopes to make a pilgrimage to the monastery itself while—"

"Some religion," said Timmy, chuckling. "A few rundown rumdum monks turning out a clunky liqueur called Cobra Tonic in a ramshackle stone ruin. They're so impoverished they had to rent the Dopestix people this plain of theirs to—"

"Orts," said Jolson.

"He says the interview's over," translated Molly for the reporter.

"It was over before I even crossed the threshold," remarked Timmy, leaving her chair and hurrying to the door. "Thank you, one and all."

"Dross," said Jolson.

Snorting, Timmy took her leave.

CHAPTER 24

There were three broad circular stages floating above the late-afternoon field. Atop each a jazz group performed, the music mixing and jumbling together and spilling down across the yellow plain. On the lowest platform, which was about five feet in the air, sat a six-armed green folksinger playing a twelve-string guitar and a chubby catwoman whapping a tambourine with her paw.

"Now, the very first time I done heard this here song," the green man was telling the audience that sat on the grass below, "it were playing on the jukebox in a diner orbiting the planet Zegundo in the . . ."

Jolson and Molly, at the edge of the small crowd, kept moving along.

On the second stage, hovering ten feet up, a toadman was soloing on an electrosax.

"Go, man, go!" chanted his audience.

Free of the performing area at last, Jolson quickened his pace and headed for the wide dusty road that led to the Monastery of Saint Viper a half mile away.

"That was Lafcadio Latterly," mentioned Molly, glancing back at the middle stage. "I had all his vidcaz albums when I was in my teens. Remember his version of 'Scrapple from the Apple'?"

"Nope."

"Darn, that's right." Catching up with him, she took hold of his arm. "I keep forgetting you're quite a bit older than I am. Things I'm nostalgic about mean nothing to you."

From a slashpocket of his throbbing cazsuit Jolson took the map of the Monastery of Saint Viper that Sniffer had produced. "According to this, we want the cell once used by Brother Jack. That's—"

"Poor little Sniffer was heartbroken at being left behind."

"Yep, I thought I noticed a catch in his voice while he was insulting and vilifying me."

"You might at least've left Starpirate's brain behind for him to guard."

"Oddly enough," responded Jolson, patting an inner pocket, "I trust myself more than I do that mean-minded mechanism."

"I'm really surprised you haven't realized that his snide remarks mask a sensitive—"

"Here's the monastery."

The place consisted of three squat stone towers linked together by smaller brix buildings and surrounded by a rock wall that had long ago started to crumble. About half the red tiles of the sloping roofs were missing, and those that remained were dingy and cracked. Several glum green pigeons were perched on the rusty rain gutters.

In the entryway, taped to the rusted bars of the permanently half-open gate, was a faded gloletter sign: *Home of Cobra Tonic! There are many imitations, but only one true*

Cobra liqueur! Tour of the Monastery & a First-Rate Blessing: $8 $3.

There were fifteen or so pilgrims and tourists in the weedy stone courtyard of the run-down monastery. They were looking over the Saint Viper Souvenir Shop, the Saint Viper Package Store and the Saint Viper Discount Sacred Relic and Holy T-Shirt Outlet. Seated at a bowlegged card table near the entrance gate was a catman monk in a much-mended tan robe and cowl.

"Sign your pledge cards, folks," he was urging the roaming visitors. "Become a satisfied member of the Friends of Saint Viper. Here's just part of what you get—a handsome T-shirt, guaranteed to fit all sizes, that depicts Saint Viper delivering his famed Sermon in the Taproom of Dusty's Bar and Grill, plus an impressive membership voxcard that not only speaks your very own name clearly and distinctly, but sings two, yes, that's two, hymns and Saint Viper's favorite drinking song. And there's more. You . . ."

Jolson escorted Molly through the modest crowd and up to the arched entrance of the monastery building.

As soon as they crossed into the shadowy corridor a plump toadman monk appeared from out an alcove. "That'll be eleven trudollars," he said, extending a green hand palm upward.

"Tripe," said Jolson.

Molly interpreted. "Mr. Poison wishes to know what the eleven is for."

"It's the standard pilgrimage fee. But if this is Billy Poison, then it'll be just nine trubux." He tilted his hand, reached, shook Jolson's. "We give celebrities a discount of thirty percent off and so—"

"Dross."

"Billy thinks you're only giving him twenty percent."

"Bless my bones," said the green monk, slipping a small calculator from within the voluminous sleeve of his robe, "I do believe he's right. Yes, yes . . . what you have to pay is only seven-seventy. And keep in mind you're getting the deluxe pilgrimage. You're able to visit three, that's right, three, sacred shrines, the cell wherein Brother Bob was visited by the vision of—"

"He's more interested in viewing the cell of the fabled Brother Jack."

The monk took a step back, jingling the ring of keys hanging from his belt. "Ah, now, there I'm afraid I'm going to have to disappoint you nice people," he said. "We've stopped including that in our tours, because of some nagging plumbing problems. However, you will be able to see our tasting room and, at no extra charge, have a sip of Cobra Tonic, a free biscuit and—"

Zzzzzummmmmmmmm!

Holstering his stungun, Jolson caught the toppling monk. He propped him in the alcove in a praying position, borrowing his ring of keys. "Let's get on with this pilgrimage," he told Molly.

Shivering, Molly hugged herself. "I can see where you'd have mystical experiences all the time in a cell like this," she observed as she followed Jolson into the eight-foot-by-eight-foot windowless cell of the late Brother Jack. "There's obviously nothing else to do."

He was studying the map again. "Our hound's printwheel seems to be in need of repairs. The lettering on this is fuzzy and—"

"Sniffer hand-lettered that." Molly seated herself on the low bench against the far wall. "It was sort of cute the way he held the pen in his little paw, concentrating, his little tongue poking out between—"

"Starpirate remembers this cell being larger than it is." He squatted on the chill stone floor. "So his recollection of exactly where he buried the Saticoy political archives may well be cockeyed too."

"You all just do the best you can, son, and—"

"Hunz Hungerford." Looking toward the open doorway, Jolson started to rise. "The Political Espionage Office's crackerjack—"

"Don't even think of reaching for your old gun," advised the heavyset human who came into the small cell, a kilgun in his fat left hand. He was about Jolson's age, pale and wearing a three-piece white bizsuit. There was a distinct limp when he walked, and his broad forehead was dotted with perspiration. "Howdy, Miss Briggs. Right nice to meet up with you."

Jolson said, "Hungerford, the PEO can't interfere with the legitimate business of a legitimate detective agency that—"

"You must be Ben Jolson underneath that persona," said Hungerford. "In the first place, as you ought to know, son, PEO agents can do just about any old thing they dang please. 'Nother thing, I'm sort of on my own just now, aiming to gather up all this here Saticoy material and use it to further my financial growth and political career."

"That's a violation of the PEO oath of—"

"Darned if it ain't," agreed Hungerford, smiling. "Now, if you'll go right ahead and unearth all them valuable documents Mr. Jackland Boggs, aka Starpirate, hid away, I'll be right obliged to you."

"How'd you come to show up here?"

"I had a tip—one that cost me a pretty penny—that Boggs had stashed the stuff somewhere in these parts," replied the renegade PEO agent. "I been hanging around hereabouts near to a week, seeing could I pick up some specifics as to the exact location." Laughing, he scratched at his ample midsection with his free hand. "There I was standing out there in a field and listening to Lafcadio Latterly—boy, when I was a kid I had all his vidcaz albums—and then who should go traipsing by but cute little Miss Molly Briggs. Since I knew she was working on the Starpirate case, I upped and tailed the little lady. Figured as how you must be one of her tame ex-Chameleons."

"PEO isn't going to take kindly to your branching out on your—"

"Jolson, I can just as like use that little old map of yours after you're dead and gone," mentioned Hungerford. "Thing of it is, for old times' sake, since we once both worked for PEO, I don't want to do you in. But you best start digging up them documents right quick, son."

Jolson exhaled, carefully. "The stuff is supposed to be under the sixth stone from the east wall in the fifth row from the north wall."

"Miss Molly, would you, please, get up off that pretty little butt of yours and count that off for us."

"You aren't doing," she said, not moving, "your reputation any good by—"

"Shake a leg, honey, or I'll shoot Jolson."

Molly stood and said, "Give me the numbers again."

"Sixth stone from that wall on your left," said Hungerford. "Fifth row from the wall you're facing."

Watching her feet, Molly started counting. After a moment she stopped and pointed down. "This ought to be it, oughtn't it, Ben?"

"Next one over."

"Don't you go trying no tricks, you hear," cautioned the erstwhile PEO agent.

Jolson knelt. "You can see this stone's been futzed with recently."

"All right now, son, you just pry it up nice and easy."

Using only his fingers, Jolson got the flagstone lifted free of the floor. There was a two-foot-deep hole beneath it. "Empty," announced Jolson.

"Huh?" said Hungerford.

CHAPTER 25

Keeping his kilgun aimed in Jolson's direction, Hungerford performed an awkward sideways squat. "Now, ain't that something," he remarked while probing the empty hole with pudgy fingers.

Jolson watched him. "You sure you didn't drop in here earlier, Hunz?"

"Shucks, now, I got better things to do with my time than stage morality plays for galactic gumshoes." With considerable effort he got to his feet and stood puffing. "Appears like we got us some rivals, Jolson. Would you and this pretty little lady have any notion as to—"

"Grab yourself some air, blimpy. And drop the weapon."

Stiffening, the pale Political Espionage Office agent started to turn.

"Drop the roscoe right now or I'll fry your goonies," warned Sniffer from the threshold.

"Doggone, but you got a funny voice for an operative," said Hungerford, tossing his kilgun into the hole in the floor.

"Frisk him, Benjy."

While doing that Jolson mentioned, "You were supposed to be confined to quarters, Snif." He relieved Hungerford of a stungun and an electroshiv.

"Leaping hyenas," remarked the robot dog. "Had I remained in that mobile cesspool, you'd have been rendered defunct about now by this large economy suetball who—"

"Well, what do you know?" The disarmed man swung around and got his initial gander at Sniffer. "Outsmarted by a little bitty old toy pup that—"

Zzzzziiinnnnnnn!

A thin beam of greenish light came sizzling from Sniffer's left eye. When it touched Hungerford's knee, he gave a pained yowl and commenced hopping.

"Darnation, son. That's right painful." When he ceased his jittering, he stood massaging the attacked kneecap.

"If you hadn't dropped the gun on time," said Sniffer in a pleased tone, "I could've directed that into your rucksack, fatboy. And keep in mind that you have experienced but one of my myriad concealed weapons. Act accordingly."

"Lordy me, how can you stand working with this little old wiseass gadget, Jolson?"

"It's a chore."

Sniffer trotted over to the hole. "The object of our quest has seemingly flown the coop." Lowering his head, he sniffed.

"We were," said Jolson, "in the process of discussing that very fact, Snif, when you intruded into—"

"Intruded and saved your toke, yet again, may I—"

"Fellas," cut in Molly, "we've got bigger problems. For

instance, we have to find all the darn Saticoy material. Since it isn't here, we—"

"I'm nearly certain, from my astute reading of Starpirate's brain, exactly who made off with the goods," Sniffer told them. Settling onto his haunches, he addressed Hungerford. "Are you aware, lardbarrel, that Brother Jack composed ninety-seven sermons and four hundred and one epistles while rooming in this bleak wickiup?"

"I don't see as to how that has a—"

"During your stay you may be able to accomplish even more."

Zzzzzzuuuunnnngggg!

The beam this time was yellow and originated in the dog's right eye. As soon as it hit Hungerford's chest, the chubby man fell asleep.

Catching him as he drifted snoringly toward the stone floor, Jolson dragged him over and laid him out on the bench. "Do you really have any idea who beat us to the Saticoy papers, Snif?"

"Geeze, not so much as a 'Thank you, Sniffer,' after I thwart that lunkhead and—"

"Thank you, Sniffer. Who?"

"You have but to follow me." The robot dog trotted out into the stone corridor. "I'll lead you to the answer."

Molly's nose wrinkled as she followed in the wake of the robot dog. "What's that you're supposed to be doing, Sniffer?"

"Skipping," he replied, continuing to skip along the long, dim stone corridor of the monastery.

"He's being elated," explained Jolson. "To a low-grade

artificial intelligence such as Snif possesses, these tiny triumphs of—"

"My tiny triumph, rinky-dink, towers over any and all of your cheesy achievements on this particular caper," Sniffer said, bounding up a stone staircase. "Once again proving that a good little robot can beat a big numbskulled humanoid with—"

"You really have to work at learning to be diplomatic," Molly told the capering hound. "It's not nice to go around—"

"We've arrived." Sniffer nudged the thick neowood door at the top of the stairs with his nose.

A metal plate affixed to the door announced *Chief Executive Monk—Brother Gill.*

The door swung open inward with a mild creaking. In the office beyond was a neowood desk, and seated straight and stiff behind it was a glassy-eyed catman in monk's robes.

"Bless - my - soul - if - it - isn't - Brother - Sniffer," droned Brother Gill. "It-is-a-joy-to-see-you-again-my-son."

Leaning an elbow on the pedestal that held a small statuary depiction of Saint Viper delivering his Sermon to the Brewery Workers' Annual Picnic, Jolson inquired, "What did you use on this guy, Snif?"

"Hypnobeam, one of many handy gimmicks built into my right forepaw." The robot dog hopped up into the visitor's chair facing the stupefied holy man. "I guess, Molly, I never quite got around to telling you that our chum Starpirate and Brother Gill here were cronies. Fact is, this fuzzy gent knew all about where the political tidbits were stashed. When the Monastery of Saint Viper fell on hard times—make that harder times, since this dump's been on hard times for many a moon—when that happened, Brother Gill decided to try to make a buck off the Saticoy materials."

" 'Twas-a-miracle," droned the robed catman. "Saint-Viper-himself-appeared-to-me-in-a-mystical-vision. It-was-quite-something. Colored-lights-and-celestial-voices. The-upshot-of-it-was-we-were-to-use-these-shameless-documents-to-finance-our-continuing-good-works."

"Blackmail," amplified Sniffer. "Even as we speak, a couple of saintly goniffs named Brother Buzz and Brother Jerry are off working a scheme to raise some dough."

Jolson asked, "Where'd they head?"

"Seems they're headquartered in the capital city of Jazinto Territory."

"Back where I started."

"That's where we'll have to go," said Molly.

"Bless-you-on-your-journey," intoned Brother Gill.

CHAPTER 26

After the televator materialized Jolson on the fifty-ninth floor of the Hotel Elegant, he paused in the plum-colored corridor to pluck a pinkish plyochief from the breast pocket of his two-piece magenta bizsuit. Dabbing delicately at his short yellow beak, he started for the door of suite 59A, murmuring, "Oh, my. Oh, my. Such a terrible experience."

He tapped at the door with a gloved hand, taking a few more swipes at his beak before returning the plyochief to its pocket.

"Yeah?" said the voxbox mounted in mid-door.

"My goodness me," said Jolson, patting his little feathery face with gloved fingertips, "I realize I'm awfully late. The most annoying thing has—"

"Who the heck are youse?"

"Oh, my, yes, forgive me." From a side pocket he took a voxcard.

"THIS IS TO INTRODUCE JAMES PEARLY ZYNEPHRINE," shouted the talking business card, "CONFIDENTIAL SECRETARY TO SENATOR BASCOM!"

"Youse had an appointment for an hour ago, jocko."

"Don't I just know that, my, yes. But then, and I assure you it was a complete surprise to me, my landcar broke down in a highly unsavory part of town while I was en route here and, well, what with one thing and another I'm only now arriv—"

"Hold it whiles I check with the two Holy Rollers," the door told him.

A moment later the door slid aside and a plump, nearly bald human stood beaming beatifically out at Jolson. He wore the robe of the Order of Saint Viper. "What's this we hear about your having car trouble, Mr. Zynephrine?"

"Yes, well, it was quite something. . . . Are you Brother Jerry?"

"I am Brother Buzz. Do come in."

The parlor of the suite was done in silver and black.

"Even though I am awfully tardy," said Jolson, pulling out his plyochief to dab again at his beak, "I am prepared to conduct whatever business is necessary, Brother Buzz. The senator is willing to pay any reasonable price for that embarrassing series of tri-op photographs of him cavorting with several members of Troop Twenty-six of the Galactic Skyscouts and—"

"My son, a slight hitch has developed," said the monk, glancing at the closed silvery door across the room. "We have an unexpected visitor this morning—a Miss Frances S. Firestorm, who happens to be the executive secretary of the International Brotherhood of Grafters. This young lady, a rather aggressive titian-haired beauty, is in the process of making us, Brother Jerry and myself, a quite substantial offer for *all* the Saticoy materials. That would include, I fear, the entire set of rather loathsome pictures of your employer and that bevy of obese young men."

"My, oh, but this is most unsettling news indeed." Jolson crossed to the silver door. "However, I am prepared to negotiate in this matter. Perhaps I can outbid this pushy young woman and yet—"

"My son, I don't think it wise to intrude at this—"

"Ah, but I'm most anxious to settle this." Jolson opened the door, entered the den.

A lean human monk was sitting on a Lucite love seat. Flame Flenniken, wearing a sedate two-piece emerald-green skirtsuit, was atop his lap and talking into his ear.

"Well, well," said Jolson, both gloved hands fluttering, "I fear I can't offer the same incentives that my rival can. No, indeed."

"Um," said Brother Jerry, removing the red-haired impostor from his lap and placing her beside him on the love seat. "Um . . . Yes, Miss Firestorm and I have just about reached an agreement. Therefore we won't be able to deal with you, Mr. . . . ?"

"Zynephrine." Jolson sat, uninvited, in a tin armchair facing the two of them.

From the doorway Brother Buzz said, "Mr. Zynephrine claims he's fully prepared to outbid the young—"

"It's not just a question of money." His colleague retied the thongbelt of his robe.

Leaning back, Jolson smiled a small birdman smile. "I can't help but, my gracious, wondering as to what the young lady can possibly pay you with—for the money part of the transaction, I mean."

Flame glared at him. "Listen, twit, the International

Brotherhood of Grafters has a hell of a budget for just this sort of deal and—"

"Yes, to be sure, I know they do," he acknowledged, resting his left arm on the arm of his chair. "The point I was making, you see, is that you don't happen to be their executive secretary. No, my gracious, you are none other than Flame Flenniken, the notorious space pirate. Therefore, you—"

"Flimflammed," realized Brother Jerry, moving as far from her as he could without leaving the chair.

"Flummoxed," said Brother Buzz, staring at the redheaded pirate.

"Okay, fellas, we'll get to this sooner than planned." From her purse she grabbed out a kilgun. "Since this feathery twerp is wise to me, I'll just take the Saticoy stuff and—"

"I assume your recent remarks to me were all falsehoods," said the saddened Brother Jerry.

"Each and every one, yeah."

"And you really don't think I have a sexy nose?"

"That one was especially untrue," admitted Flame.

Very casually, Jolson used his Chameleon abilities to elongate the arm that was dangling over the edge of his chair. He sent his hand snaking unobtrusively along the ebony rug and behind the nearby love seat. "Goodness, Miss Flenniken, I should think you have more than enough horrid crimes on your record already," he said, right hand fluttering in the vicinity of his beak. "Surely you don't wish to add the slaughter of a pair of men of the cloth to the list?"

"Pipe down, my son," urged Brother Buzz. "Don't go

putting ideas in her head. She hasn't as yet mentioned killing any—"

"I sure don't need this twit to give me that idea, Buzzy." Flame gestured at him with the kilgun. "Fact is, unless you fellas fetch the—Awk! Oof!"

Jolson's fist had come rising up over the back of the love seat to deliver three powerful disabling blows to the base of her skull.

Sighing, gasping, the lady space raider fell forward, hit the floor, the kilgun cartwheeling up into the air out of her lax fingers.

On his feet, Jolson caught the gun before it fell. He gave the fallen Flame two more blows to the back of the neck.

After reeling in the arm he'd used to disable her, he knelt to tie her wrists behind her supple back. "Now then, gents," he said upon rising.

"A miracle, I do believe," exclaimed Brother Buzz, bringing his plump palms together. "Did you witness, Brother Jerry, how this man's arm stretched and stretched until, taking this vixen completely by surprise, he—"

"Quit playing the simp, Brother Buzz," advised the other monk. "He's obviously a Chameleon Corps agent or some such and the game's up so far as we—"

"The Saticoy stash," requested Jolson, pointing the confiscated kilgun first at Brother Jerry and then at Brother Buzz.

"Ah, my son, I fear you won't be able to commit the sin of grand theft," said Brother Jerry, tapping his fingertips together. "We had that material locked away down in the hotel safe upon checking in here to commence our fund-raising for the good of Saint Viper."

"I already had a chat with the manager of this place,"

Jolson informed him. "Used a very effective truthdisc. He tells me you have all the stuff in a safe here in your suite. Safe's behind a painting of Saint Viper delivering his famous Sermon to the Bouncer at Sharky's Bar and Grill."

"Perhaps we could discuss a sharing of—"

"Keep stalling and your nose is going to be even less sexy."

Exhaling forlornly, Brother Jerry said, "I can see there's no use arguing with a man who would hijack the church."

"None at all," agreed Jolson.

CHAPTER 27

Jolson, himself yet again, punched out an automatic landing pattern on the dash. "There's Preston Zuck's cottage down below," he said as the rented skycar dropped down through the afternoon sky to go skimming over the dozens upon dozens of pleasant white cottages that made up the Tranquility Village sector of the territorial capital.

Loosening her safety gear, Molly leaned over to kiss Jolson on the cheek. "Well, this case is just about tied up, Ben, and you've done a terrific job for BIDS," she said, smiling and kissing him once more. "Oh, yes, sure, you let our original client get murdered, and that's probably going to scare off hordes of clients. On the other hand, though, if we garner a testimonial from a contented customer like Preston Zuck, it could possibly lure that many customers in. So, gee, we—"

"Can just about break even."

Sailing over the white picket fence surrounding Zuck's white cottage, the skycar landed itself on his pink gravel driveway. The vehicle bounced twice, coughed, was still.

"Actually," said Molly while gathering up the attaché

case Jolson had acquired at the Hotel Elegant and climbing out, "I keep trying to look on the bright side. Except for poor Maybelle Vexford, really, things went fairly well. True, she ended up a bloody corpse, but otherwise we did—"

"Had I but taken Sniffer along when I called on her, the dear lady might well still be alive today." He joined her on the path to the front door. "Then we wouldn't be calling on her agent but on—"

"You tend to take simple statements of fact as nasty criticisms of you as a person, whereas . . . darn, plaz." She'd stopped to pick one of the daisies that grew beside the bright green lawn and discovered it was artificial and firmly moored.

Jolson continued on, climbed the three red-painted neowood front steps and rang the doorbell.

After a few seconds a husky blond man opened the door, thrust out a beefy hand. "Hiya, pal, put 'er there." His grip was strong.

"Mr. Zuck?"

"That's right, buddy. I'm Preston Zuck, literary agent. C'mon in, bring the chick."

Molly held up the attaché case by the handle. "We have everything you hired us to find, Mr. Zuck."

"Hey, that's swell, babe." He patted her on the backside as she and Jolson entered the cozy parlor of the cottage. "Park your toke anywhere it suits you. I'll dig out the old checkbook."

Frowning slightly, Molly sat in a sudochintz armchair and crossed her long legs. "You've changed some, Mr. Zuck."

"Listen, sister," he said, grinning and nodding Jolson

down into another of the chintz chairs, "I got wise to myself." He dropped onto a sudochintz sofa. "This is an old-fashioned, conservative planet. Nothing like Barnum. Hell, a bozo can be gay there and who's to care. Here on Esmeralda, though, it's still rough. So I've decided to modify my image." He spread his arms wide. "More manly now, don't you think?"

"Well, yes," said Molly, tapping her fingers on the attaché case full of Saticoy material that rested across her lap. "Although you maybe have gone too far over on the other side, by a little anyhow."

Jolson was sniffing the air. "We'll also turn the Jackland Boggs brainchip over to you, Zuck, and—"

"Something wrong, Jolson? Naw, c'mon, level with me. Acting manly is new to me, but you've had years of experience with impersonations. Any tips on what I'm doing wrong'll be apprecia—"

"Mostly it's your perfume," Jolson told the chunky literary agent. "Much too delicate."

"Hell, that's only my after-dep lotion, fella," said Zuck. "Stevedore's Dream they call it. Smells damn virile to me. What do you say, Miss Briggs?"

"Actually I can't smell a thing, so—"

"Hey, anyway, I really got a boot when you pixphoned to tell me you got the brainchip and all the Saticoy material," said Zuck. "Once Jackland Boggs gets the chip installed in his conk, why, he can get cracking on the autobiography. I've already arranged to hire one of the best free-lance hacks in the universe to take over for Maybelle. Big guy named José Silvera—know him?"

"Met him once or twice." Jolson grinned amiably, reaching into his jacket. He brought out a small object, jumped up, lunged and slapped it against the literary agent's thick neck. "That's a truthdisc, Wally."

"The perfume, huh?" said the now mind-controlled man.

"Same stuff you were wearing when you were Jody Pearl up in The Islands."

"I've got a real fondness for that scent—it's got a passion fruit base—and I keep dabbing it on me even when I'm working."

"Where's the real Zuck?"

"Back in his bedroom, stungunned."

"I'll go revive him so we can get to business."

"Almost got you, didn't I?" said the ex-Chameleon Trumbower. "And I thought the acting manly was neat—audacious, too. Hell, any nitwit can swish around, but to do a nance who's trying to be butch, that's a brilliant touch. Calls for—"

"Sit in silence." Jolson crossed to the doorway. "Watch him and the Saticoy stuff, Molly. I'll bring Zuck back with me."

"I think my nose must be plugged up or something," she said. "I never noticed his scent at all."

The true and authentic Preston Zuck blinked and sat up on his pink quilted comforter. "Dearie me, I'm all aflutter," he said, shaking his head cautiously from side to side. "It's my impression, kind sir, that you've rescued me from some frightfully dire plight."

Jolson put his drugkit away, saying nothing.

"You seem thoughtful," noticed the revived literary agent, smoothing at his maroon lounging pajamas.

"I was trying to decide which version of you I like better."

"I don't quite understand what—"

"Molly Briggs is here with me. We have the brainchip as well as the—"

"If it's all the same with you . . . Mr. Jolson, isn't it? If it's all the same with you, Mr. Jolson, I'd rather not work with her. After the sneaky way she came into my cottage at, I swear, the ungodly crack of dawn, and used a really vulgar stungun to—"

"Nope, that wasn't Molly," Jolson told him. "Just an ex-Chameleon named Wally Trumbower."

"It's all very confusing to—"

"If you're up to walking—or even tottering—I'll get you to the parlor, Zuck. Then we can turn over everything to—"

Zzzzzzuuuummmmmm!

Someone had fired a stungun up in the parlor.

Tugging out his own stungun, Jolson started for the doorway.

"Don't come out of there with any weapons showing, Jolson," warned a familiar voice, "or I'll shoot you dead."

The highly polished right arm showed around the doorjamb. "Come on out where I can see you, Jolson," requested Lieutenant Hillman of the Territorial Police Murder Squad.

After a few seconds Preston Zuck called out nervously, "Dearie me, Lieutenant, it really seems as though you're laboring under a misapprehension. There's absolutely no one in here except—"

"Spare me the crap, Zuck." The bulky cyborg appeared in the doorway.

Clutching the comforter up around him, Zuck said, "You have my solemn word that—"

"What's a book agent's word worth?" Chuckling, Hillman entered the bedroom. "I've had this damn cottage bugged for days, which is why I know for sure that Jolson and the Briggs bitch arrived here about twenty minutes back." He was glancing around the room.

"Why, whatever gives you the right to spy on—"

"Relax, I'm not at all interested in what you and your boyfriends do here by night," the policeman assured him. "Where's Jolson hiding?"

Inadvertently the literary agent let his gaze go to a closet door across the bedroom. Guiltily, he looked suddenly at an opposite wall.

Chuckling again, Hillman came over and sat down in the chintz armchair beside the bed. He turned it so that he could watch that particular door and Zuck at the same time. His metal arm rested across his knees. "Let me explain what's going to be happening here."

"Really, Lieutenant, I suggest you take your leave. I'm not without influence in this—"

"Naw, killers don't have much influence with anyone."

"Were I a killer, that might—"

"Hey, you are, Zuck. Sure, you're a multiple murderer," explained Hillman, aiming his metal forefinger at the closet door. "Today alone you're going to slaughter three more people. Yeah, you're a brutal guy."

"Three *more?*" I assure you, I've never so much as—"

"You forget that you knocked off Maybelle Vexford—

after cleverly jobbing her vidscan camera so it wouldn't show your arrival or exit and only that of the phony Dr. Chowderman," said the cyborg cop. "That can be done, you know, if you're on to a few tricks of—"

"That," realized Zuck, letting the comforter drop away from his chest, "that's actually what you yourself did, Hillman. You went to Maybelle's that night and—"

"Sure, right." Lifting his metal hand, he aimed at the door again and sighted with his thumb. "I'd heard rumors about Starpirate's brain being missing and that Vexford had important information on that whole business. So I dropped in, tried to get her to talk. She was a hell of a lot tougher than I thought and she started to go for a gun herself." He shrugged.

Zuck shook his head. "But she . . . from what Miss Briggs told me . . . Maybelle muttered about Dr. Chowderman as she was dying."

Laughing, Hillman said, "I was lucky there—so were you, Jolson. She told him something like 'I thought he was Dr. Chowderman.' Now Jolson, having ex-Chameleons on the brain, he assumed she was alluding to the fake Dr. Chowderman. But what she was saying—and remember that people who are dying aren't always crystal clear in their conversation or thinking—was that she was expecting a visit from this fake Chowderman. And when she heard me coming in unannounced, she called out, 'Is that you, Dr. Chowderman?' Fortunately, she switched to the topic of where Balooka had gone. I was hiding in the next room, and if she'd mentioned me, Jolson would've been dead and done for, too."

Zuck almost glanced toward the closet door again, but caught himself in time. "One of my other authors is actually at work on a proposal about crimefighting. I can hardly believe that she intends to devote an entire chapter of this proposed book to your career."

Hillman shifted in the chintz chair. "Being greedy for Starpirate's loot doesn't mean I'm not still a good detective," he said. "Hell, you have to be good to work all this out. Sure, I let Jolson and all these other bastards go busting their balls all across the planet, looking. I simply tapped all the likely places they'd bring Starpirate's brain or the loot. I wait patiently, taking no risks at all. Then I move in and collect." He stretched his metal arm out further. "I was sort of betting on you, Jolson. I figured you'd find Starpirate's brain before any of the others."

Zzzzzzzaaattttt!

A crackling beam of ebony light leaped from his metal forefinger, ate a large hole in the closet door. And then two more at different positions.

"Oh, Lieutenant," gasped Zuck, "you've—"

"No, Zuck, *you've* bumped off Jolson. A shame, since he wasn't a bad operative if you could overlook all his wiseass remarks. But that's the— Damn!"

The arms of the chintz chair had moved, tightening around the seated cyborg and pinning his arms to his sides.

"Now's the time to use the stungun, Zuck," ordered the chair.

"I really have a dreadful aversion to weapons of—"

"Use it. Now. And aim true."

"Yes, very well, yes." The agent reached under his pillow, dragged out Jolson's stungun and pointed it at the pinioned Hillman.

"You better not shoot me," warned the cop, "or I'll—"

Zzzzzzzzuuummmmmmmm!

Hillman stiffened in the chair, then slumped. The chair opened its arms and he toppled over onto the floor.

Jolson changed back to himself and, naked, walked to the closet. He reached through the lowest hole, felt around and located his clothes. "You did a good job of diverting him, Zuck," he said. "Hillman really thought I was hiding in here."

Watching the ex-Chameleon dress, Zuck said, "Back in college I was quite active in the drama department. I usually played the leading lady. You were a very convincing chair, I might add."

"I won't work in drag," said Jolson, "but I have no objection to upholstery."

CHAPTER 28

Out beyond the tinted glaz windows of the spaceport restaurant a liner was lifting off. It went roaring up, trailing fire, into the gathering dusk.

"It's awesome," said the husky, clean-shaven green man. "Yes, I never cease to be inspired when I contemplate the grandeur of travel through space. The gleaming ships laden with happy wayfarers and rich cargoes, bound for the myriad exotic ports of call this wondrous universe teems with and—"

"Are you ready to order?" inquired the thin birdwoman waitress of the green man.

He was sharing a circular glaz table with Jolson, Molly and Preston Zuck.

"Boggs wanted to see you off," said the agent, "so that he might convey his gratitude at—"

"I'm on a low-xibble diet, sweetheart," Starpirate informed the waitress. Reaching into the breast pocket of his conservative three-piece grey bizsuit, he brought out a pair of old-fashioned spectacles. "Take the other orders while I look over the menu screen again." Putting on the glasses, he hunched and moved his crewcut head closer to the display screen in the tabletop.

"I'll have, I guess, the sinsteak," said Molly, watching Boggs.

"Choice of arugula, fiddlefern, koksaghyz or snerg for vegetable," said the waitress.

"Snerg's an animal," mentioned Jolson.

The waitress sighed. "I missed today's briefing. Excuse it."

"Arugula, I suppose," said Molly absently.

"What'll the botanist have?"

Jolson grinned. "Soy loaf sandwich on Plutonian Soldier's Black Bread."

"We're out of Plutonian Soldier's Black Bread."

"Hellquad Sailor's Whole Wheat, then."

"Dearie me, I'm not at all hungry," said Zuck. "What's the soup of the day?"

"Snerg broth," answered the waitress, brightening. "There, I knew we had snergs on the menu someplace."

"Does that come with free crackers?"

"No."

The agent considered. "Oh, I'll have it anyway."

Starpirate said, "Just bring me a cup of warm water and a thin slice of Martian Civilian's White Bread gently toasted."

"What a feast." The waitress departed.

Molly glanced again at Boggs. "I guess I have to ask you this," she said. "I can understand why they shaved your head, Mr. Boggs, but why the beard?"

"Beard was my own idea," he replied, settling back in his chair. "Now that I've embarked on a literary career, I decided to change my image. No more the ogre, but from now on the gentleman. I've modified my vocabulary as well."

Zuck said, "I've tried to explain to him that this is all wrong for the talk shows and the lecture circuit. People expect space pirates to be great, sweaty, uncouth fellows with all sorts of unkempt hair. A looter who looks more like a galactic public accountant than a—"

"Dignity means more to me right now than bestsellerdom." He tapped his temple. "I want to thank you and Ben Jolson, Miss Briggs, for getting the brainchip back for me. And I've got to tell you, it works better than the original brain. Why, the clarity of my current—"

"At least with the old one," said the agent, "you behaved in an acceptable scourge-of-the-spaceways manner. Like someone I could get the media all excited about."

From another pocket of his suit Starpirate took an envelope. "This is to be split between you and Miss Briggs, Jolson." He passed the envelope across.

Taking the envelope, Jolson opened it and looked inside. "A Banx check for five hundred thousand trubux," he said. "Thanks, Boggs, that's—"

"Think of it as a bonus," Starpirate said.

"Five hundred thousand." Molly frowned. "I don't know if we ought to accept such—"

"Of course we ought." Jolson slipped the check away into a pocket.

Molly was sitting in the least comfortable chair that her spaceliner cabin had to offer, a stiff unyielding thing constructed of metal tubes and thin strips of hard neowood.

Her elbows were poking into her knees, and her chin rested in her cupped hands. "Darn," she observed.

Jolson was slouched on the jelsofa, his back to the small oval viewindow that showed the vast emptiness of space they were hurtling through. "You feel like this at the close of every case," he reminded her. "A certain amount of letdown is—"

"You're right, yes. I know."

"Meditate rather on the extra five hundred thousand we got from—"

"I know, I know."

"Why, by the way, were you so reluctant to take money from Boggs? With your orientation, I expected—"

"Mostly because he's such an unsavory person," she answered. "I mean, when we were supposedly going to work for poor Maybelle Vexford, that seemed okay. Even working for Preston Zuck didn't make me uneasy. When the scourge of the spaceways, though, hands the dough directly to you—money that's come from looting and pillaging the cosmos—that gives one pause."

Jolson grinned. "Sometimes, Molly, you're not hard-boiled at all," he said. "Yet both heredity and environment ought to have—"

"Would you mind moving to that other sofa, the rubberoid one yonder?"

"Nope. But why?" He rose, causing the jelsofa to sway and yawp, and walked to the purple sofa. He sat.

Standing, Molly replied, "Because I want to sit next to you for a while, but I don't like those squishy sofas at all. Makes me feel as though I'm the topping on a dessert." She sat down beside him.

Jolson put an arm around her shoulders. "What you

have to strive to do," he advised, "is not let the people we encounter cause you—"

"Darn. I wish I hadn't made a rule about not fooling around with you."

"Someone in an executive position such as yours can modify or waive the rules."

"Okay, but just for the duration of this trip, or until I get over the blues," she said. "Whichever comes first."

"Understood."

"Somehow, at the conclusion of each case, I start finding you particularly attractive."

Something fell over in the shut closet across the cabin, producing a dissatisfied bonging noise. "It's bad enough being locked up in here," complained the voice of Sniffer. "But must I also listen to this romantic piffle?"